"Let's scare Jenny to death. . . .
The thrill of the game
is in the playing. . . .'

"Wait," she pleaded. "You're going too fast."

She made herself concentrate on Derreck now, on his flashlight aimed ineffectually at the tunnel floor, the way he blended so perfectly with the shadows, slipping in and out of them so easily, so expertly, almost as if he didn't care that she was following *. . . almost as if he's trying to lose me. . . .*

He stopped so abruptly, she didn't see him.

He grabbed her arms and shoved her back against the wall, and as she opened her mouth to protest, his hand clamped down over it with frightening strength.

"If it were up to me, I'd have you out of here in a second!" he hissed. "You don't belong here—you have no business going *anywhere* in the castle, understand? And if it takes fear to get you to leave . . . then I promise you . . . your nightmare's just beginning!"

Books by Richie Tankersley Cusick

BUFFY, THE VAMPIRE SLAYER
(a novelization based on a screenplay by Joss Whedon)
FATAL SECRETS
THE MALL
SILENT STALKER
VAMPIRE

Available from ARCHWAY Paperbacks

RICHIE TANKERSLEY
C U S I C K

Silent Stalker

AN ARCHWAY PAPERBACK
Published by POCKET BOOKS

New York   London   Toronto   Sydney   Tokyo   Singapore

This book is a work of fiction. Names, characters, places, and incidents are either the product of the author's imagination or are used fictitiously. Any resemblance to actual events or locales or persons, living or dead, is entirely coincidental.

AN ARCHWAY PAPERBACK *Original*

 An Archway Paperback published by
POCKET BOOKS, a division of Simon & Schuster Inc.
1230 Avenue of the Americas, New York, NY 10020

ISBN: 0-671-79402-7

First Archway Paperback printing April 1993

10 9 8 7 6 5 4 3 2 1

AN ARCHWAY PAPERBACK and colophon are registered trademarks of Simon & Schuster Inc.

Cover art by Gerber Studio

Printed in the U.S.A.

IL 7+

Especially for Sarah Janicke . . .
I love you, Sarah Girl

Silent Stalker

1

Looking back, Jenny realized she should have listened to the warning.

She should have believed what Nan was trying to tell her and stayed far, far away from Worthington Hall.

But danger was the last thing on her mind that wet June night, traveling in the old Chevy with Dad, wishing she could be anywhere but where she was. And who would ever have thought—even guessed—that a simple vacation was destined to turn out the way it did?

All Jenny was aware of that particular evening was how miserable she was, and how thunder rumbled off in the distance, threatening more rain at any second, and how she'd never seen such terrible fog in her life, swirling the air in stringy gray waves, drizzling down between thick canopies of leaves overhead as her dad coaxed the car farther down the muddy dirt road.

"We're lost, aren't we?" Jenny shivered. "Castles are big—it's not like you can just hide a castle in the woods and not see it."

"Patience, patience," Mr. Logan murmured, leaning closer to the windshield. His hair fell stubbornly over his wire-rimmed glasses, making him look every bit the absentminded writer he was. "It's a *rebuilt* castle. A *smaller* version of the Worthington family's ancestral home. If I remember my information correctly, a lot of the building materials came straight from the original castle in England."

"All right, a *smaller* version. But there's still supposed to be a medieval fair on the grounds," Jenny added. "Do you see any signs of a fair? Do you see *anything?*" She nodded uneasily at the darkness beyond her window. "It's been twenty minutes since we left the main road, and we haven't met a single car. If there's a fair going on, and some castle to see, then where are all the people?"

"The fair would be closed by now, I expect." Dad glanced quickly at his watch and sighed. "Nearly nine, can you believe it? And I told Sir John we'd be here to interview him by seven." He sighed again, hunching his shoulders. "This has to be the right road. . . . I took the turnoff he told me about. . . . He had us come in the back way, a more direct route to the house. . . ."

"Maybe he's planning to have us ambushed and robbed." Nervously Jenny glanced out again at the trees pressing close on either side, the black restless shadows slipping past as the headlights strained uselessly into the tunnel of darkness ahead. *Oh, Mom, how could you do this to me? Dad and I were like total strangers while you two were married— what made you decide things could be any different now since the divorce?*

She sat up straighter as they rounded a curve, and a pale shaft of moonlight wavered down across the road in front of them. Like a ghostly vision, a stone gatehouse arched high over the road, and as Jenny gazed at it in surprise, a tall shadow pulled slowly from a niche in the wall and calmly blocked their way, keeping just beyond reach of the headlights.

"Ed Logan," Dad said amicably, whipping out his wallet to show identification. "I'm writing a feature on fairs and festivals in America. I believe Sir John's expecting me."

A flashlight flared and spotlighted his driver's license, then just as suddenly turned full force onto Jenny's face. Immediately she dropped her eyes, but when the glare persisted, she tried to pull away from it against the door.

The flashlight followed her.

It moved over her face, then crept past her shoulders and played slowly across the front of her T-shirt.

"Dad," Jenny whispered, hugging her arms around her chest.

"Hmmm? Oh." Mr. Logan looked up from his wallet as if he'd just remembered she was there. "My daughter, Jenny. I hadn't planned on bringing

3

her, but . . . umm . . . something came up. Unavoidable. I hope Sir John won't mind. She'll be helping me with my research. Sort of."

The light pulled back and angled sideward, but all Jenny could see was the yawning gateway before them.

"Okay?" Dad tossed his wallet onto the dash. "Okay to go through now?"

There was no response. As Jenny inched forward and peered out her father's window, she felt her breath catch in her throat. Through a dimly lit patch of swirling fog, she could see two eyes gleaming back at her, but where a body should have been, there were only shadows.

"Dad," Jenny whispered again.

Without warning a circle of light swept out in front of the car's hood, motioning them forward. As Mr. Logan inched the car toward the arch, Jenny turned in her seat to look back. She didn't notice the sudden movement in the trees beside the road. She only heard the loud thud against her side of the car as the back door burst open and someone jumped inside.

"You're going the wrong way!" a girl's voice hissed. "Don't you know? You'll never come out . . . never again!"

Mr. Logan slammed on the brakes, and as Jenny turned around, the flashlight beam stabbed straight through her father's window once more, pinning the face over her left shoulder.

At first all Jenny could see was hair—long stringy mats of it—but then, as the girl leaned forward between the seats, one dirty arm lifted to fend off the glare, and a pair of wide, dull eyes blinked at Jenny through the tangles.

"He'll like you," the voice quivered. "I know. You have to leave! Before it's too late!"

Jenny guessed the girl to be about her own age, yet the poor thing's face was so scratched and streaked with dirt, it was hard to tell for certain. Her tattered blouse hung loosely off her shoulders, and there were places on her arms that looked like dried blood.

"Who are—" Jenny began in alarm, but without warning the guard's arm shot through her father's window and clamped mercilessly onto the girl's upraised hand. In the half light all Jenny could see was his black sleeve and one black glove and his fingers squeezing the girl's thin wrist until she whimpered in pain.

"Leave her alone!" Jenny cried. "Dad, do something!"

"You'll be sorry." The girl bent close to Jenny, her lips moving against Jenny's ear. "He'll kill you. I swear."

For just an instant the terrified eyes gazed full into Jenny's face. Then the girl yanked free, scrambled from the car, and promptly disappeared into the darkness.

The glove pulled slowly back.

As Jenny peered after it into the shadows, she saw nothing but black, endless night.

"They certainly believe in putting on a show, don't they?" Dad chuckled, giving Jenny a wink as he started the car slowly forward again. "Great place! Close that door, will you?"

Jenny stared at him, then turned in her seat and pulled the door shut. She looked behind at the road. There was absolutely no sign of the guard . . . or the girl.

As if no one had ever been there at all. . . .

"What do you mean, part of the show?" Jenny's voice shook, and she paused, trying to get control of herself. "Didn't you see that girl's face? She looked really *scared!*"

"Of course she did—she's an actress." Dad chuckled again. "All the people you'll see working at the fair will be acting—that's the whole point of everything!"

"What point?" Jenny said irritably. "What are you talking about?"

"That girl had a costume on, Jenny, didn't you notice? I've read all about these fairs—don't be surprised if *everyone* has an English accent and goes around in medieval clothes!" Mr. Logan pushed his glasses up the bridge of his nose. "And don't expect any of these people to step out of character as long as tourists are around. That's what makes it so believable! Going back in time!"

Jenny sat stiffly in her seat, her mind racing. *Actress!* But Dad hadn't looked into the girl's eyes the way Jenny had, hadn't recognized the fear there—the panic. *She couldn't have been acting. She seemed too terrified. . . .*

"Didn't you hear what she said to me?" Jenny tried again, but Dad was pointing out the window.

"There's your castle," he announced. "Hiding here in the woods after all."

Jenny gasped and sat forward, her hands clutching the dashboard. And for just an instant the thought came to her that she must be having a strange sort of dream, only she knew she couldn't possibly have fallen asleep. . . .

Worthington Hall rose up through the fog, its ominous silhouette etched against a backdrop of thickening stormclouds. Somber and watchful, it stretched deceptively into the surrounding darkness, its crenellated towers shimmering ghostly beneath a sudden glimpse of sickly yellow moon.

"Is it . . . is it real?" Jenny heard someone whisper, and then realized with a start that it was her.

"Well," Dad said, "there's only one way to find out."

"You have to leave."

Jenny glanced at him quickly. "What?"

"I didn't say anything."

"Oh. I thought . . ." She let her fears go unspoken, keeping her eyes upon the huge monstrosity as they drove closer. Now she could make out more turrets and battlements, massive trees clawing high up the old stone walls, and dark slitted windows warily watching their approach. . . .

"Leave . . ."

"See? Maybe it wasn't such a bad idea your mother had, you and I spending this summer vacation together," Dad said offhandedly, bouncing the car over the deep ruts in the road. "I know you had plans with your friends this summer, but I

7

could sure use a secretary—sorry—*assistant* for this project, and it might as well be you. It's just that I've been working so *hard.* . . . I really *meant* to keep in touch with you a lot more since the divorce, but—gosh, things have been so busy and your mother's not the easiest person to communicate with and there's always my work and—"

Here it comes, Jenny thought grimly—*all the old excuses, the same old reasons he's always too busy to care.* . . .

"Dad," Jenny said, changing the subject, "let's not talk to Sir John tonight, okay? Let's just find a motel—"

"Jenny, you know we can't—we just checked every motel in town, and there aren't any vacancies. I don't know why I didn't think to make reservations earlier—"

"Then let's go on to some other town and come back tomorrow when the fair's going on—"

"What?" Mr. Logan looked at her as if she'd lost her mind. "Turn back now? Are you kidding? I'm just beginning to realize I came here for the wrong story. I should be doing something on this great old *house!* How can you even think about waiting till tomorrow? Look at this place—doesn't it just thrill you with a sense of history and tradition?"

But those weren't the words Jenny would have chosen. As the car slowed once more, she gazed up at the sheer walls of the castle and felt only a heavy sense of foreboding.

"Is that a drawbridge?" she asked weakly, but Dad was already maneuvering across the heavy wooden planks. Jenny looked down into a shadowy suggestion of water far, far below and tried to keep from shuddering. As they continued through yet another gatehouse, they found themselves in a huge empty enclosure completely surrounded by high stone walls.

"Well, that's strange," Dad mumbled, turning off the engine and opening his door. "We're obviously in a courtyard, but there doesn't seem to be anyone around. Maybe they decided we weren't coming till tomorrow after all, and everyone's gone to bed."

Jenny got out reluctantly, letting her gaze travel around the enclosure. If Worthington Hall had looked threatening from a distance, now it looked positively nightmarish—a cold, invincible cliff carved from the depths of the night. Here and there torches cast flickering shadows from niches on the walls, and as Jenny turned in a slow circle, she noticed yawning doorways and stone stairs appearing at intervals, all recessed deeply into the walls with only empty blackness beyond.

"Dad, let's go," Jenny pleaded, but her father was already walking toward one of the staircases, waving back at her over his shoulder.

"Maybe nobody's home," Dad joked. "Only ghosts."

Jenny started after him. Around her the air moved restlessly, sending tendrils of fog across her cheeks, and she could swear that the night had turned suddenly cold. As a clap of thunder exploded some distance behind her, she whirled just in time to see a jagged spear of lightning split a tree

9

beside their car. With a resounding crash, one of the huge limbs toppled onto the hood, crushing the whole front end.

"Dad!" she shouted. *"The car!"*

Mr. Logan didn't answer.

Jenny turned back to where he'd been standing, but her father had disappeared.

2

*D*ad!"

As Jenny stood there in disbelief, the sky opened up, gushing torrents of rain. In a matter of seconds the hard-packed ground beneath her feet turned to slime, and she was soaked clear through to her skin. *He was there—I saw him just a second ago—something must have happened—*

"Dad!" Jenny·shouted again, but her voice was lost in the rushing downpour. "If you're trying to scare me, please stop! This isn't funny!"

Rain closed her in on every side, as thick and dark as the fog. She could scarcely even see the car anymore, and it was all she could do to fend off a wave of hysteria. Swallowing a sob, she ran toward the stairs where her father had been headed and ducked gratefully beneath an overhang, pausing a moment to catch her breath and pull her wet hair out of her eyes. Most of the torches had gone out, but this one near the staircase still burned. As her gaze moved slowly up from the floor in front of her, she counted five steps before they vanished into total darkness. *I can't—I don't know what's up there. What am I going to do?*

She closed her eyes and took a deep, shaky breath.

"Well, well," the voice said in her ear. "What have we here?"

Jenny started to scream but felt a hand clamp over her mouth.

"Not a good idea," the voice scolded gently—a soft voice, definitely male. Jenny struggled but couldn't turn her head. She could feel his body, tall and strong against her back, and when he spoke again, he sounded amused. "Do you know what we do to trespassers around here? We torture them."

A fresh surge of panic went through her. She twisted, but he only held her tighter against him.

"You might as well stop struggling." He laughed. "It won't do you any good. And it just might make me angry."

Jenny stopped. She could feel her heart hammering in her chest.

"This won't do at all," he said, his voice lowered. "I believe I can hear your heart racing. In fact . . . I swear I can actually *see* it beating right through your . . . clothes."

In spite of her terror Jenny's cheeks flamed. She stiffened as his hand relaxed . . . hesitated . . . then drew away from her lips.

"Now," he said. "Let's get a proper look at you."

Furious, Jenny whirled around, a string of insults

12

ready on her lips. And then, as she looked up into his face, her heart fluttered straight into her throat.

In the flickering torchlight she saw the delicate contours of his face, his high cheekbones, his perfectly formed lips. The wind had tousled his wild dark mane of hair, yet his eyes shone down at her with an unexpected kindness and calm. As the light played over his body, Jenny could also see the blousy white shirt he wore loose over tight black pants, the boots that rose snugly to his knees, his tanned fingers resting casually on the wall above her head. Framed there by the walls of the castle, he conjured up every legend Jenny had ever heard about knighthood and chivalry and romantic heroes.

"I—I—" she stuttered and saw a smile ease across his lips. "You—"

"My lady." To her surprise, he gave a deep, sweeping bow, then straightened up again with a look of undisguised amusement. "Whatever shall I do with you?"

"Where's my father?" was all she could manage in her most indignant tone.

"Your father?" This time when he spoke, his bewilderment sounded almost convincing.

"I'm Jenny Logan." She bit her lip to keep from shouting. "My father was just here, and now he's disappeared! We came all this way, and now look at our car and—" She broke off abruptly, struggling to keep her voice under control as the young man stepped closer.

"Ed Logan is your father?" he murmured, but before Jenny could answer, his arm moved in a wide arc, indicating the staircase. "You'd better come with me."

Jenny's knees felt weak. She wasn't sure she could walk, but as he climbed the steps and disappeared into the darkness, she had no choice but to follow. Her head was reeling between anger and relief. She could hear his steps ahead of her, echoing sharply on stone, yet she couldn't see any sort of light. As she stumbled and nearly fell, he caught her elbow and sighed.

"My apologies. I know the way so well."

To Jenny's relief a flashlight snapped on, illuminating the floor at her feet.

"Who are you?" Jenny demanded. "And where are you taking me?"

The beam reflected dimly off the stained, slimy walls, and she could see his face again, could see how the corners of his mouth twitched. "Malcolm Worthington. And since you're a trespasser, where do you *think* I'm taking you?"

Jenny balked, but he reached out and gently shook her shoulder.

"I'm joking. Although . . . you might be surprised how enjoyable some tortures could be."

Again Jenny's cheeks flamed. She thought she heard him chuckle as he continued on, and she hurried to keep up. They seemed to be going through an endless maze of winding tunnels. She could feel slippery drafts of damp air, and she shrank from the wet stone walls around her. As Malcolm turned a corner without warning, Jenny suddenly found herself alone in an intersecting passageway, and she stopped in confusion, calling into the darkness.

"Malcolm—wait! I can't see you!"

Her own voice echoed back at her mockingly. She thought she heard the fading sound of footsteps . . . then nothing.

"Malcolm!"

Jenny fought off a surge of panic. As she stood there in pitch blackness, she clenched her arms around herself, terrified to reach out, terrified of what she might feel. . . .

"Malcolm . . ." Her voice sank to a whisper. "Please don't leave me. . . ."

Close to her side she sensed a subtle stirring of shadows . . . felt a whisper of stale air creep slowly over her face. . . .

Jenny knew she wasn't alone.

As a scream rose into her throat, she felt icy fingers touch the back of her hair . . . move across her neck . . . and slide slowly down her spine.

3

J enny!" Malcolm's voice shattered the darkness. "Jenny, where are you!"

The fingers uncoiled . . . slid away . . .

"Jenny! Answer me!"

As Jenny's terrified cry echoed on and on through the tunnel, she felt other hands grabbing her shoulders, and she screamed even louder, beating out at them with her fists.

"Stop it, Jenny!" Malcolm wrestled her arms down to her sides, pinning her tightly against him. "It's me—stop it!"

"Didn't you see him!" Jenny babbled. "Didn't you? He touched me! He tried to—"

"What? Calm down, I can't understand a thing you're saying—"

"You must have seen him—you *must* have! He had ahold of my neck—he—you *had* to see him—"

16

"Jenny, I can barely see *you*—and now you've made me drop the flashlight and break it, so we'll have to go on in the dark."

"I'm not going *anywhere!* I want my father and I want to *leave!*"

Jenny could hear a deep sigh in Malcolm's chest as he fought for patience.

"All right, then, shall I just leave you here and go off to find this father of yours?"

"No! Don't you dare leave me again!"

"That's what I thought." This time his shoulders moved in a gentle laugh. "These passages are old and filthy, Jenny. It was probably just spiderwebs you felt. Or these awful drafts. They'd make anyone imagine ghosts." Jenny closed her eyes. Malcolm's heart was beating beneath her cheek, warm and solid.

"It's just that . . . it seemed so real. . . ."

"And now you know why everyone was so superstitious all those years ago," Malcolm said. "With shadows and dampness and . . . things hiding in the night . . ."

Was it her imagination or had his voice sounded troubled for just an instant? As the silence dragged out, Jenny felt his arms tighten around her briefly before they pulled away again. "Come on." Malcolm's voice floated eerily in the dark. "Hold on to me, and I'll walk slow."

"Are you sure you know the way?"

"With both eyes shut."

As Malcolm's fingers closed around hers, Jenny remembered the icy-cold touch of that other hand and tried not to cringe. *I must have imagined*

17

it. . . . it was only a draft, like Malcolm said. He would have heard something . . . he would have known . . . Trying not to think about it anymore, she blindly followed Malcolm's lead. It was so dark, she couldn't even make out his shape ahead of her, yet she could definitely feel the passageways becoming more twisted. *How do I know he's taking me to Dad? Suppose he's leading me completely away—Dad won't even miss me until it's too late—*

"Ah. Here at last."

Jenny hadn't realized he'd stopped. As she plowed into him, Malcolm steadied her with his free arm.

"Where are we?" Jenny demanded. She could feel him pushing her away, but she was afraid to turn loose.

"The great hall. Where I believe your father is enjoying his dinner."

"His dinner?"

Without warning a door creaked open, revealing a sudden burst of softly flickering torchlight. It was a huge room, wide and long, hung with tapestries and shields and the stuffed, mounted heads of wild animals. A fireplace took up one entire wall, and as Jenny moved cautiously forward, the sweet fragrance of herbs drifted up from the rush-strewn floor. Several dogs skulked into corners as she passed, but though they cast her wary looks, they didn't seem particularly interested. Approaching the raised dais at the end of the room, she not only recognized her father at the oversize table there, but realized there were three other people sitting

and talking around him, their faces indistinguish-
able in the throbbing lights and shadows from
many candles.

"Father," Malcolm announced, steering Jenny to
the base of the platform. "It seems we have an
unexpected . . . visitor."

"Jenny!" Mr. Logan exclaimed cheerfully, looking up from his plate. "Oh . . . have you been outside all this time? This is Sir John. Sir John, my
daughter."

The room went silent. As Jenny paused beside
the dais, she had the unsettling impression of eyes
creeping over her, stares emanating from the deep
wells of darkness around the table. Shadows flickered up the walls as seconds dragged into endless
minutes.

"Daughter?" It was an elderly voice which spoke
at last from the head chair. Jenny heard its cool,
smooth tone, its guarded politeness, and felt an
unexpected shiver up her spine. "I don't recall any
mention of a daughter, Mr. Logan."

"Right. My wife's idea. Well, ex-wife," Dad
clarified, shrugging his shoulders. "Quality time,
get to know each other—that kind of thing."

Same old Dad . . . Jenny stiffened at her father's
indifference; she opened her mouth angrily, but he
rushed on.

"She won't be any trouble, Sir John, I promise
you that. In fact, she'll be helping me with my
notes."

Again the heavy silence . . . the slow inspection
by hidden eyes . . . as if whoever else was there,
concealed in the shadows, had suddenly held his

breath. Jenny wanted to turn, to run, but could only stare helplessly as Sir John leaned forward into the candlelight.

"She shouldn't have come—" a voice began from the other side of the table, but the old man cut it off with an abrupt gesture and raked Jenny from head to foot with his eyes.

"Lovely," the old man murmured. "So very . . . lovely. Come closer."

Jenny felt Malcolm's hand on her back, nudging her forward. She could see Sir John more clearly now—his startlingly gaunt face, silver hair flowing to his shoulders, silver goatee upon his chin. As she stared back at him, he squinted down at her, much like a predator gauging its kill.

"Well done, Malcolm," he murmured. "Well done, indeed."

"But she shouldn't be here." Again the voice in the shadows spoke; again Sir John dismissed it.

"What my other son is trying to say, Miss Logan, is that girls—forgive me—young *women*—are a rarity at Worthington Hall. Sit there."

"Excuse me—" Jenny began, but Sir John shook his head.

"I did just say *sit,* did I not? Or am I a total fool?"

"No, my lord, *I'm* the fool," another voice piped up. "You're merely senile."

There was an undercurrent of laughter, and to Jenny's increasing discomfort, a jester suddenly popped out from the shadows along the wall, the belled tassels on his cap jingling merrily. He had a cute, boyish face, and eyes that crinkled up to match his mischievous grin, and as Jenny backed away, he leapt lightly onto the table and squatted on his heels, looking down at her.

"A game!" the jester announced. "So *many* of us—and only one Jenny. Who will win her heart?"

Nervously Jenny realized that Malcolm had seated himself at the table, leaving her alone on the floor.

"I saw her first,"—Malcolm winked—"so by right—"

"Or by wrong . . ." The jester swept his arm in an inclusive gesture. "Make your choice, my lady."

Jenny was speechless. She stared at the jester and saw him stretch slowly toward her.

"Wit." The jester offered Jenny a handshake. "At your service." She hesitated, unsure what to do. Finally she extended her own hand, but he snatched his fingers away, his grin widening.

Jenny flushed, more from anger now than embarrassment.

"Dad"—she fought to keep her voice calm—"I think we should—"

"Wit," the jester said again, pointing to himself. "And Malcolm." He indicated the young man who had rescued Jenny, and as Malcolm gave her a smile, Wit continued introductions around the table. "Sir John. And the infamous Derreck."

At the last name another face materialized from the shadows, and Jenny caught her breath sharply. He had Malcolm's face, Malcolm's clothes, even the same amused smile on his lips. Confused, she glanced back at Malcolm and saw both of them turn their heads toward each other, the exact same movement at the exact same moment.

"Twins." Wit sighed. "Poor Malcolm. Poor Derreck. They're beside themselves."

As everyone laughed, Jenny looked helplessly at her father, who was obviously enjoying the whole bizarre scene.

"Do join us, my dear, and forgive our little eccentricities." Sir John indicated the end of a bench, and Wit jumped down to pull it out, landing lightly as a cat. "We have an insatiable passion for games."

Jenny hesitated, wondering if Wit would yank the seat out from under her, but he only winked and slid her smoothly up to the table.

"This *house* is a game, actually," Sir John went on. "My pet whim . . . my indulgence, if you will. Full of secrets . . . mysteries . . . things that are *not* what they seem to be. We've *always* been very fond of puzzles, haven't we, Wit?"

"To be sure." Wit gave a wry grin. "We're a very—puzzling—family, my lord."

Jenny risked a glance around the table. Derreck, Malcolm, and Wit were all watching her, and as she shifted uneasily, she saw a secretive look pass slowly from each of them to the other and back again. She dropped her eyes and felt an inexplicable panic rising in her chest.

"If it's human interest you're after," Sir John said casually, "you've certainly come to the right place. I'm sure you'll find more than enough . . . atmosphere . . . to satisfy your creative curiosity."

"Right down to the family curse," Wit said dryly.

Sir John stared at Wit with a cold, humorless smile.

"Unfortunately, lightning's just brought a tree down on top of their car." Malcolm broke the silence, pushing a platter of food toward Jenny, but she shook her head.

"Really?" Mr. Logan looked amazed at the news.

"Nasty business, that," Sir John remarked.

"A truly crushing experience," Wit added.

"I don't suppose we could stay the night?" Mr. Logan announced cheerfully, leaning back with a smile. Jenny looked at him, incredulous, but he rattled on. "With this damn storm, and everything booked up in town—well, you know, I was just telling Jenny, I think the *real* story here is this house! I mean, talk about human interest! We could stay here and get some information on your castle and work the fair at the same time! But, hey, wait, I'm being rude here." He looked properly chastised. "Inviting myself like this—what can I say? Hey, forget it. Of course it'd be great publicity for you—but I don't want to be out of line, okay? If we could just stay tonight, then tomorrow I could get the car taken care of, and Jenny and I can find a place to stay farther down the road."

A heavy silence settled over the table.

From the corner of her eye Jenny could see Derreck and Malcolm staring down at their plates. Finally Sir John shifted slightly in his chair, his voice carefully polite.

"Of course you'll stay over, Mr. Logan. How

inconsiderate of me not to offer sooner. We wouldn't think of turning you out on a night like this."

Jenny looked wildly at her father. He was positively beaming.

"It'll be great for the feature," Mr. Logan said, nodding eagerly. "Being here . . . getting a real feel for the place."

Still the boys said nothing. Jenny heard Wit clear his throat, and she knew she wasn't imagining it this time—that quick, furtive glance passing from each of them to the other.

It wasn't a look of welcome.

"And where will we . . . put the girl?" Derreck asked slowly, raising an eyebrow at Jenny.

"Jenny," Wit corrected, but he wasn't looking at her, he was leaning toward the fireplace, and the flickering light made strange, distorted patterns over his face. "Long blond hair, sweet blue eyes," he murmured, "unsuspecting to surprise—"

"You need practice," Sir John broke in. "Your poems make no sense."

"Don't they?" Malcolm whispered.

Again there was a long moment of silence. Sir John sipped thoughtfully at his glass before he finally spoke.

"The tower, I should think." He picked up a crystal decanter . . . reached toward Jenny . . . paused when she shook her head no. "The tower should be . . . adequate."

"The tow—" Malcolm began, but Wit's elbow dug into his side, and he clamped his mouth shut.

"That's really so nice of you, but we wouldn't

want to impose, would we, Dad," Jenny said hopefully. She started to get up, but Sir John's hand shot out and caught her arm. She flinched as he pushed her back down in her seat.

"No imposition, I assure you." Sir John smiled. "I only hope you won't find your visit ... uneventful."

4

"You're being a brat," Dad said under his breath as he pulled their suitcases from the car. "You're upsetting me."

"Because I'm scared to stay here?" Jenny sounded stunned. "How can you say that? Excuse me, but didn't you notice anything weird going on in there?"

She watched as he walked off several feet, then turned back to face her, his expression angry.

"Just like your mother," he snorted. "Always trying to ruin my plans—"

"Is there a problem?" Malcolm shouted. "Do you need some help? Hurry—it's starting to rain again!"

Jenny glanced over to where he and Wit were waiting in one of the doorways of the courtyard.

"Please, Dad," she whispered, "let's *leave!*"

But her father had already stalked away, and as she picked up her suitcase, her heart sank into her stomach.

"A damsel in distress if ever I saw one," Wit murmured to Jenny as he hurried over to take her bag.

"Sorry about the rooms." Malcolm's eyes shifted from Jenny to her father as they headed into the castle. "We weren't expecting company, so I'm afraid you'll have to stay in separate wings of the house."

"What has smelly wings and flies?" Wit demanded.

Malcolm gave him a look. "We don't want to know."

"Worthington Hall on a hot summer day."

"You're beginning to annoy me." Malcolm shouldered past him. "And hold that light so they can see where they're going."

The four of them wound through yet another maze of corridors and finally stopped outside a heavy wooden door. Malcolm ushered Mr. Logan in and pointed back toward the passageway.

"Derreck's room is just there on the other side of those stairs," he said. "And a bathroom, as well. I wouldn't go wandering round on my own if I were you—some of these doors open into absolutely nothing, and some of the steps are so worn, they're only good for falling down."

Jenny couldn't hear her father's reply. She watched as Malcolm closed the door and rejoined them.

"Yours is a much nicer room." He gave her a smile. "Lots more private."

"That's a delicate way of putting it," Wit said.

"You're making me stay in a tower?" Jenny asked uncertainly. "You mean a *real* tower—somewhere up there?"

She glanced toward the staircase, but Malcolm shook his head.

"No, not there. We don't use that wing of the house. It's . . . closed off." Wit was staring at him, but Malcolm didn't seem to notice. "You'd better use the bathroom here if you need to, before we go on."

Jenny went inside and shut the door. She felt trapped. As she opened her suitcase on the bathroom floor, she could hear Malcolm and Wit speaking softly in the hall, but she couldn't understand what they were saying. She ran the tap water as hard as it would go, then pressed her ear against the door.

"—believe it," someone mumbled. Wit, she thought.

"—have to be careful—" *Malcolm?*

"—seen him yet—"

"—you know—locked—but locks mean nothing—"

The voices stopped. Uneasily Jenny drew back from the door and finished at the sink.

Stepping out into the corridor, she was surprised to find it deserted. She pressed back into the bathroom doorway and scanned the hall slowly from end to end. Sconces flickered high up on the walls, and the long passage throbbed with shadows. *Like it's breathing . . . like it's alive.*

"Malcolm?" she whispered. "Wit?"

There was no answer.

Jenny gripped the door with one hand and lowered her suitcase to the floor. *What am I worried about? Dad's room is just down that other hall. I can run . . . I can scream . . . He'll hear me—*

They were playing a joke on her. That was it, she tried to reason with herself, that was the whispering she'd heard while she was in the bathroom—they'd been planning some way to scare her, and they were probably hiding right now, watching her, getting such a kick out of seeing her terrified—

"I know you're there"—Jenny tried to control the trembling in her voice—"so you might as well come out."

And even as she was speaking, she saw something stir within the shadows at the far end of the passageway, something slip behind the huge tapestry hanging there, so that it billowed faintly along the floor. . . .

Jenny started toward it.

She didn't want to, but she knew there wasn't a choice. If she didn't face up to the boys now, she'd be at the mercy of their tricks her whole stay.

I'll sneak up and scare them . . . That'll make them think twice about picking on me anymore . . .

She was closer now . . . only ten feet away.

Close enough to see the tapestry stirring again— *it is moving, isn't it?*—beckoning her. . . .

And suddenly she could see something . . .

something barely showing just beneath the fringe at the bottom . . . *a foot?—a shoe?*

"Jenny, where are you going?"

With a scream Jenny whirled around to see Malcolm and Wit staring at her from the opposite end of the hall. As her eyes widened, she whirled back again, but the tapestry was hanging straight and still, nothing but floor underneath.

"Sorry . . ." Malcolm hurried to her side as Wit picked up her bag. "Father needed us, and we didn't think you'd be out so soon."

"I—I thought I saw something." She pointed, and Malcolm looked in the direction of her finger.

"There?" He nodded. "A tapestry. Yes, it's very old."

"But it was moving," Jenny insisted. "Almost like—"

"I told you, these damn drafts." Malcolm glanced at Wit, who just as quickly glanced away, and the three of them continued to the end of the hall. Jenny took a last suspicious look at the tapestry as she turned down a smaller corridor, then Malcolm opened another heavy door and began leading the way up a winding flight of narrow stone steps.

"Wait." Jenny paused, realizing she was sandwiched in between the two boys. "What's up here?"

"Your room." Malcolm's voice sounded hollow and strange echoing off the encircling walls, and Jenny reluctantly started forward again as Wit pushed her from behind.

"But it's so"—her eyes took a quick, frightened inventory as they started up—"so damp. So . . . I don't know . . . abandoned. I don't want to stay in the tower—"

"And why not a tower?" Wit retorted. "Aren't princesses *supposed* to live in towers?"

Flustered, Jenny saw Malcolm smile as he reached back to take her hand. His fingers closed tightly around hers.

"Careful," he warned. "Don't trip."

Jenny gave him a vague nod. The passage was so narrow and claustrophobic that she shrank away from the walls and tried not to touch the stones on either side.

"There's a reason it winds this way, you know," Malcolm spoke up, noticing her revulsion. "Stairwells went to the right, to make it harder for attackers to draw and use their swords. See? You've no idea what might be waiting for you just round this curve."

Jenny raised her eyes nervously. The stairs kept winding and winding, as if they would never end.

"You don't really live here, do you?" she asked, trying to control the quivering in her voice.

"At Worthington Hall?" She could see the shrug of Malcolm's shoulders. "Not since we were small. It was one of the easiest things of our childhood to leave behind."

"So all of you are—"

"Brothers, yes. Derreck, of course, and Wit."

"Worthingtons of a feather flock together," Wit chanted.

"Supposedly our mother died right after Wit was born." Malcolm held the torch high and glanced back at her, his face in half shadow. "Although we strongly suspect he was *abandoned* on our door-step—"

"I was a changeling," Wit said mournfully. "And I kept on changeling every year. . . ."

In spite of Wit's attempt at humor, Jenny shuddered. "I can't imagine growing up here. Weren't you terrified?"

"Terrified?" Malcolm laughed. "A castle and a pack of rowdy boys?"

"Boys will be boys," Wit said philosophically. "They can't very well be girls."

"Can you even imagine a more wonderful fantasy?" Malcolm went on, ignoring him. "This whole place was like one huge playroom. We all knew the castle like the backs of our hands, didn't we, Wit?"

Wit stuck the back of his left hand in front of Jenny's face and wiggled his thumb. "I believe we turn this way."

Malcolm reached a small landing and made a sharp turn to the right. "Our great-grandfather originally built Worthington Hall. From stones and timbers torn down from the family castle and then shipped here to America. The castle was already falling apart—he couldn't afford the taxes or the upkeep—"

"But he was a loyal Englishman," Wit said dramatically, "and he wanted part of his homeland with him."

"He sold the land for quite a bit of money, and moved what he could of the house. Worthington Hall eventually passed on to his only son. Grandfather and then Father after him kept on building, even after we went away. So I suppose there could be lots more secret passages and rooms we don't even know about. The place is honeycombed with tunnels underneath. An honest to goodness maze."

"Which delights Father no end, I'm sure." Wit's tone was bland, and Malcolm threw him a knowing look.

"You've seen it, too, then—the way he acts. He's gotten a bit . . . peculiar . . . even Derreck said something about it."

Wit's head moved in a faint nod. He raised an eyebrow in Jenny's direction, and Malcolm immediately turned his attention forward again.

"You said you went away," Jenny pursued, interested. "Why did you leave here?"

"He sent us," Malcolm said. "He *sent* us away to school."

"Boarding school?" Jenny asked, and Wit gave a snort.

"In hopes we'd all return to keep the home fires burning. Can you even imagine it? Coming back here to dedicate your life to this rotting monstrosity?"

"So what do you do now?"

Malcolm seemed to find her question amusing. "Not very much. Together, that is. It's not so easy to keep in touch anymore, with all of us scattered in different directions."

"What he means is," Wit explained, "we're totally worthless. The lot of us."

"Unmaterialistic," Malcolm corrected. "That has a much nicer ring to it. Derreck works construction. I work my way through Europe whenever I get half the chance. And Wit"—he sighed indulgently—"lives alone on the beach with his paints and brushes."

"I'm a starving artist," Wit spoke up. "I live right on the ocean. Get my drift?"

"I'd live anywhere," Malcolm mumbled. "Anywhere in the world but here."

"Liar," Wit challenged him. "You wouldn't live *near* the ocean—you're afraid of water."

Malcolm glanced back at Jenny with an apologetic shrug. "I can't swim."

"And your father's never wanted to leave here?" Jenny asked.

Malcolm hesitated . . . glanced back at her over his shoulder. "No. He'll probably die here, in fact. Just fade into the walls and become one of the venerable old stones."

"A worthy end. A worthy match." Wit hopped up three steps on one foot. "They go so well together. They even look alike—or haven't you noticed?"

An edge of uneasiness went through Jenny. She tried to turn the discussion away from Sir John.

"So," she said pleasantly, "are all of you here for the fair?"

Their silence was sudden and guarded. Malcolm hesitated on the step above her, and Wit stopped abruptly behind.

"We were *summoned.*" Wit's tone was mocking.

"Father's growing frail, you see," Malcolm said slowly. "He can't keep the place going—"

"He's growing *crazy,* you see!" Wit made circles with one finger at the side of his head. "And the older he gets, the more impossible he is."

"We're only here temporarily," Malcolm said. "We don't much care for . . . inconveniences."

"And Father is the biggest inconvenience of them all." Wit gave a snort. "He *hates* guests—he positively *loathes* outsiders."

Jenny jumped as he grabbed her free arm and leaned toward her with a conspiratorial whisper.

"Which is why you should stay *in.*" He nodded solemnly, and Malcolm laughed.

"Forgive us, Jenny. All this rambling on and on about things that don't concern you—"

"But could," Wit cut in, and his gaze shifted past her onto Malcolm. "Keep alert, brother," he said quietly. Jenny felt goosebumps over her arms as Malcolm coaxed her forward again.

"I feel so terrible for what Dad did back there," Jenny spoke up, glancing between the two boys. "Especially now that you've told me how your father feels about having guests. Dad's not the most tactful person in the world. Sir John should have just thrown us right out."

"But don't you know why he didn't?" Malcolm feigned surprise at Jenny's distress. "He never could resist a pretty face."

He and Wit exchanged winks as Jenny dropped her eyes in embarrassment.

"Worthington Hall's become hideous, really," Malcolm went on, grimacing at the dark oozing stains along the walls. "It's ridiculously expensive to maintain and impossible to clean—even if Father *could* afford decent help. The truth is, he's been forced to open the castle for tours, to ward off his creditors. He's rented out the grounds for the fair, and once that's over, tourists will start trampling through these crazy old ruins."

Jenny heard the bitterness in his voice but said nothing.

"Ah, well. Times change." Malcolm sighed. "And there's no help for it, is there?" He paused once more and smiled down at her.

"How many rooms are in the house?" Jenny asked.

"I used to know." Malcolm shrugged. "I don't anymore. But the tour will cover most of the main ones—the great hall, several of the towers, one bedroom, I believe, and the chapel."

"And the dungeon." Wit gave an evil laugh.

"Oh, yes, of course the dungeon." Malcolm nodded.

"A real dungeon?" Jenny's voice dropped, and Wit grabbed her other hand, startling her.

"With *real* instruments of torture!" he hissed.

Jenny was eager to change the subject. "Isn't there any electricity in the castle?"

"Sorry, no, not in this part," Malcolm replied. "But lots of candles. What's wrong? Don't you think it's romantic?"

"Is mine the only room? Will I be alone up here?"

Without answering, Malcolm stepped aside, steering Jenny past him out into a circular chamber. In the torchlight she could make out vague shapes of a fireplace, a rug, a bed and table, a trunk, and one tiny window. Wit moved swiftly with his matches, placing candles about, until the room finally pulled together into one complete picture.

Jenny turned in time to see Malcolm put his hand on the latch. "Is there anything you need before we go?" he asked her.

"I—" Again her eyes made a quick sweep of the room, to the two boys preparing to leave. "I—I don't think I want to stay here. I think I'd rather stay downstairs and—"

"Unfortunately"—Malcolm glanced at Wit, who immediately melted into the darkness beyond the threshold—"this is the only empty bedroom in the castle that's inhabitable at the moment—all the others are being repaired. I'm sorry we didn't know you were coming, or we'd have made it a bit more comfortable. But you're safe up here. See—there's a bolt on your door. Not that you'd need it for anything," he added quickly.

Almost too quickly, Jenny realized.

He was staring at her, and yet she had the sudden impression that he'd glanced back toward the staircase, that some invisible signal had passed between him and Wit.

"Ummm . . . there might be noises during the night," he said carefully. "Unfamiliar ones. Nothing to be afraid of."

"Castle noises?" she tried to joke, glad when he smiled.

"Of course. Castle noises. What else?"

Jenny watched him move out into the shadows
... watched the door shutting slowly behind
him ...

"Malcolm," she blurted out, "can I ask you
something?"

He stopped. He turned and looked back at her,
and she could see Wit's face hovering just above his
shoulder.

"Wit mentioned a family curse," Jenny rushed
on. "What is it?"

For a moment Malcolm's eyes, Wit's eyes,
seemed to glow at her in the darkness. She thought
she heard the boys whisper, yet she couldn't see
their lips moving. It was Wit who finally spoke, a
singsong rhyme that made her skin crawl.

"They never survive at Worthington Hall—they
shiver or shriek or they take a great fall—"

"Stop it, Wit," Malcolm mumbled, but the jester
rushed on—

"They're never the same once the ghost comes to
call—when they look in his eyes and see ...
nothing ... at ... all."

As Wit ended his chant, he swirled one hand
above his head and plucked a bouquet of flowers
magically from the air. Leaning around Malcolm,
he offered them to Jenny, but she stood there,
unable to reach out or even move.

"It's true, you know." Wit gave a mysterious
smile. "They never come out the same. They never
do."

"What ... do you mean?" Jenny whispered.

"Women at Worthington Hall. They see the

ghost. They go mad. Or die. Or simply"—he jerked his hand and the flowers vanished—"disappear."

"You're trying to scare me. Malcolm—" Jenny's voice trembled, but Malcolm wasn't there anymore, only the endless dark at the top of the stairs, and Wit was swinging the door shut, its horrible groan echoing on and on and on . . .

"Good night," Wit called softly. "Sleep well."

5

Nothing in my whole life could ever be worse than this.

Jenny leaned heavily on the door, feeling sick as the boys' footsteps faded and disappeared.

I have to be dreaming—please . . .

She shut her eyes tightly, squeezing them until they hurt, praying that when she opened them again, she'd find herself back in her own bedroom at home, that this whole thing would turn out to be just a nightmare.

"Wake up, Jenny," she whispered to herself. "You've got to wake up."

She opened her eyes.

The room flickered around her in a sallow circle of candlelight.

"I'm trapped," she mumbled to herself. "I'm trapped in a tower by two weirdos who have a curse on their family."

For one second she actually wanted to laugh, but in the next, the horrible reality of her situation rushed over her in a wave of sheer panic. Before she even knew what she was doing, she had the door open—saw the black empty hole yawning open at her feet—stopped cold.

"Oh, my God . . ."

Immediately Jenny drew back, her frightened whisper echoing in the stale, damp air. She heaved the door shut and leaned against it, her heart hammering violently.

I'll never forgive Mom or Dad for doing this to me. . . . I'll never forgive either one of them again.

On trembling legs Jenny made it over to the bed and sat down. She ran one hand along the thin covers and pulled the crumpled pillow into her lap. She wrapped her arms around it and leaned forward a little, her eyes darting nervously to the narrow window. Panes of leaded glass reflected the storm outside, and from time to time a rumbling crept through the walls, shivered through the floor, as if the whole tower might collapse at any second.

Don't panic. Just take a candle and go back downstairs.

And then what? Once she got out—*if* she got out—Jenny had no idea where to go, no idea where any other rooms or people might be.

Getting up again, she made a slow tour of her surroundings, trailing her fingertips along the few pieces of furniture, along the mantel of the fireplace. A few fine threads of spidersilk clung to her hand, and she shook them away. *So where's your*

41

spirit of adventure? How many people would love a chance to spend the night in a real castle?

Jenny opened her suitcase and began to undress. For the first time she realized how totally exhausted she was, and as she pulled on her nightgown, she yawned and gave a slow stretch.

From the corner of her eye she could see her own hazy likeness pulsing up the wall . . . shadowy arms lifted in the air, shadowy head tilted back.

Jenny raised up on her toes and stretched her hands higher.

For a moment her shadow seemed to hesitate . . . to darken and thicken from some subtle play of the light . . .

Then . . . as she watched in disbelief . . . it slowly lowered its arms.

Jenny went rigid. As she saw her shadow take on a life of its own, she tried to move her upraised hands but couldn't. A dank, sluggish breeze crawled through the room, sucking at the candles. With a choked cry she finally dropped her arms and forced herself to whirl around.

The wall was empty.

The only shadows there now were pale smudges of half-light clinging to the stones, so wispy they were almost transparent.

Tentatively Jenny lifted one hand.

Nothing happened.

Turning her head, she saw her silhouette on another section of the wall, back over her shoulder.

I'm more tired than I thought. . . . Everything's going blurry on me . . .

Frowning, Jenny rubbed her eyes and moved to the bed. She shook out the blanket and lifted it high, peering under to the very foot. Satisfied, she crawled cautiously beneath it. Malcolm had been right about the noises. As she pulled the covers tightly around her and stared uneasily into the candle flame on the bedside table, she was all too aware of faint rustlings and whisperings in the shadows, sounds so tenuous yet so close that for one second she imagined the tower walls breathing around her. Forcing the thought away, she heard the far-off rumble of thunder and saw the window glow as lightning split the night sky beyond. *This is ridiculous. . . . You haven't acted this scared since you were two years old and thought monsters were hiding under the bed. . . .*

"Stop it," Jenny whispered fiercely to herself. "Stop it right—"

Another clap of thunder exploded, and she bolted upright, the whole tower trembling to its very foundations. She wondered how sturdy it really was—what if it toppled during the night and flung her straight out into the sky? *"Take a great fall . . ."* What was it Wit had sung to her before he'd left? The song about the family curse . . . some ghost . . .

"They go mad. Or die. Or simply disappear."

But I don't believe in ghosts or curses, and I don't believe Wit was telling the truth, and Malcolm was right about him being annoying. . . .

As Malcolm's face crept into her mind, she remembered his voice again, his laugh, the warmth

43

of his touch. Slowly she lay down, gazing up at the swirling shadows of the ceiling. She was afraid to close her eyes, yet she could feel herself beginning to drift. It surprised her then, when she jerked awake and saw the dying stub of candle on the bedside table. For one panicky moment she didn't know where she was or what had woken her.

Groggily Jenny looked around the room. The other candles had gone out, and the darkness was thick and close. She groped for the candlestick and held it above her head.

A soft puddle of light spilled across the floorboards. She could barely make out the shape of the door, just enough to see the bolt still in place. The shadows seemed unnaturally still . . . dark spirits holding their breath . . .

Uneasily Jenny put the candle on the table and lay down once more.

And then she heard them.

Soft sounds. Scurrying sounds. Stopping— starting—moving again along one wall, just beyond reach of the light.

Jenny sat up, one hand pressed to her mouth. She could hear them on the walls now, clicking against the stones, on the wood of the floor, tiny feet scratching, tiny high-pitched squeals, yet she couldn't see anything, anything at all, just the shadows pressing closer and closer around her bed as the candle sputtered and started to die—

"Malcolm!"

She didn't know why she called his name. She jumped to her feet in the middle of the bed and caught one last glimpse of the door as the candle went out. In total darkness now it seemed to her the sounds had magnified—had *multiplied*—more of them—*millions* of tiny claws pattering up the walls —racing in a ring around the bed—

"Malcolm!" she cried. "Somebody help me!"

She was terrified to try for the door, terrified of what might be climbing up onto the covers. She took a cautious step, and something furry ran across her bare feet.

Shrieking, Jenny grabbed for the table. Immediately her fingers brushed over something warm and squirmy, and she screamed again, somehow managing to snatch up a candle and matches. As one match flared, she could see dark shapes swarming over the floor, and she thrust her lighted candle helplessly out in front of her.

She didn't expect to see the human shadow standing at the foot of her bed.

Tall . . . silent . . . deathly still.

In the feeble light Jenny saw the vague outline of his body . . . and where his head should have been, the shapeless hood with holes instead of eyes. . . .

And I've seen him, Jenny thought wildly, *I've seen him before, I've seen him yet I haven't seen him—eyes gleaming in the dark, body made of shadows—*

As Jenny stared, transfixed with terror, he seemed to float toward her, gathering form and substance from the darkness, blacker even than the shadows that surrounded him—clothes—boots— hood—all as black as the deepest, deadest night.

And then, as he shifted yet again, she saw his arms glide upward . . . black-gloved hands reaching out to her . . . dangling a long coil of rope . . .

A hangman's noose.

Jenny's scream filled the tower.

As the ghostly figure melted back into the wall, she leapt for the door, threw back the bolt, and flung herself out onto the stairs.

someone's fingers trailed over her face, she shrieked, even as a hand pressed her mouth.

"I'll take you," the voice whispered. "Ssh . . . I'll take you to him . . ."

Helplessly Jenny realized she was being pulled to her feet, that small, thin arms were trying to hold her up. She could smell damp hair and musty cloth—could feel the sharp, delicate bones of a shoulder beneath her cheek. She tried to push away, but as a surge of pain went through her, it was all she could do not to pass out.

"Who are you?" she begged. "Please let me go."

They were moving now, slowly . . . unsteadily, and Jenny closed her eyes against the terrifying darkness. Drafts curled along the passageway, dank air seeping from deep, hidden places. She heard a creaking sound as though a door were being opened, but when she strained her eyes, she saw nothing . . . nothing at all. . . .

Then everything stopped.

From some remote corner of her brain Jenny realized they were standing still, that the frail arms supporting her had gone suddenly tense.

"What's happening?" Jenny pleaded. "Where are you taking me?"

Without warning the arms withdrew. Jenny fell heavily onto a stone floor.

"What's wrong?" Jenny cried. She groped out wildly but touched only air. "Don't go! Please don't leave me!"

It was as if she'd been dropped at the bottom of a well. Puddles of slime oozed beneath her bare legs, and her nightgown was soaking wet.

"Please!" Jenny screamed. "You can't leave me here!"

Somewhere water was dripping.

She crawled forward, then froze.

And she knew it then, just as surely as the screaming in her brain, as the icy stabbing of every nerve—*knew* that someone else was beside her—a *different* someone, a presence so close she could feel its breathing, even though the air was so deathly, dangerously still. . . .

"Who *are* you?" Her voice was half sob, half whisper. "Why are you doing this to me?"

"Make some light," a voice murmured. "Let's see her."

A tiny jet of flame spurted out of the darkness. Shielding her eyes, Jenny blinked as a candle came into focus . . . as it revealed a swirl of hazy images hovering just beyond. . . .

Black pants . . . white shirt . . . dark hair . . . ?

"Malcolm?" The candle floated toward her face. She could feel its heat against her cheek, and she quickly ducked her head. "Derreck? Is that you?"

Something touched her neck. Before Jenny could cry out, a blindfold was slipped over her eyes and secured at the back of her hair.

"Malcolm?" she whispered. "Derreck? Please . . . what are you doing?"

"Tie her up," the voice said softly.

"Oh, God . . ." Jenny's body went icy cold. Someone grabbed her arms, and she twisted away, hitting out at the air. A cold draft rushed past her, and immediately her wrists were pinned together in a grip of steel.

"Don't touch me!" she screamed. To her horror she felt rope being wound around her wrists . . . felt a final tug as the knot was fastened in place. "What are you doing! Let me go!"

Someone shoved her forward. She sprawled on the wet floor and lay there, too terrified to move. And then she heard footsteps . . . calm and deliberate . . . making a slow circle around her.

"We're going to play a game now," the voice whispered. "It's called Scare Jenny to Death."

It was a strange voice, deep and unnatural; Jenny could tell it was disguised. Beneath the blindfold, her eyes squeezed back tears. She could feel her heart pounding, and she slowly drew her knees up to her chest.

"Please . . ." she begged. "I don't want to play any game. I just want you to let me—"

"Of course we can't tell you the rules," the voice broke in. "We make them up as we go along."

"Do you even realize how much trouble you're going to be in when I tell everyone what you've done?" Jenny burst out desperately. "When I tell my father and Sir John and the police!"

For a long moment there was silence.

Then the laugh. Unmistakably amused.

"No, Jenny. I don't think so."

Without warning a hand curled around her ankle. Jenny tried to kick it away, but it began pulling her across the floor.

"No!" Jenny screamed. *Let me go!*

"In the first place," the voice went on calmly, "there are three of us, you see. So you'll have to guess which of us is which. And who is doing what." A smile lurked behind his words. "It's a clever game, don't you agree? Requires great skill. Great . . . wit."

"Stop!"

Again Jenny tried to struggle. Her head was still throbbing from her fall down the stairs . . . her body felt bruised and numb. She managed another kick, and this time her ankle slid free.

"And in the second place"—the voice sounded thoughtful—"we're *very* good at keeping secrets. So you can understand . . . this might be somewhat of a challenge for you."

"Why are you doing this?" Jenny cried.

"Because the thrill of the game is in the playing. You'll see. Only one can win. The *best* one."

The voice hesitated . . . sank even lower. Its hoarse, strange whisper echoed off the walls . . . from nowhere . . . yet everywhere.

"Don't you wonder who he'll be, Jenny? The one who hides . . . the one who watches in the dark—"

"Please!" Jenny sobbed. "Please let me go!"

"Yes . . . yes . . . you're right. We must get on with the fun, mustn't we?" The soft laugh shivered through hollow spaces. "Oh . . . but did I forget to mention the prize?"

Without warning someone grabbed Jenny's head and bent it backward.

"You, Jenny. *You're* the prize."

As Jenny gasped and tried to scream, a sweet, sickening fragrance rushed through her nostrils and down her throat, filling her head . . . her mind . . . with total darkness.

7

"Jenny, can you hear me?"

"She can't hear you."

"No, I think she's waking up—"

"She's not waking up."

"Hand me that cloth again. Get some water."

"Are you sure she's not dead? She looks dead—"

"She's not dead. The only thing dead around here is your brain. Now stand back."

Jenny could hear people talking, voices far and distant yet peculiarly close to her, and as she struggled to answer, she had the sensation of floating upward through layers and layers of clinging mist.

"She *is* waking up, I told you. Jenny? Can you talk? Can you tell me what happened?"

With an effort she forced her eyelids open and waited for reality to focus. There were two faces leaning over her, and as she moaned softly, an arm slipped beneath her head and propped her up.

"No," she mumbled, "please . . . it hurts . . ."

She felt the rim of a glass between her lips . . . cool water easing down her throat. Her head was too heavy for her neck, and there was a dull pounding that jarred her whole body with pain. She moaned and turned her face away, relieved to be flat upon the pillow once more.

"What happened?" she mumbled.

She closed her eyes, held them shut for several seconds, opened them again. Now she could see the faces more clearly: Wit and one of the twins, both of them staring down at her.

"Do you know me, Jenny? It's Malcolm."

Jenny gazed dully into his eyes. He looked worried and upset, and as he continued to watch her, Wit nudged him impatiently with one elbow.

"I can see she recognizes you. That burst of excitement on her face."

Malcolm ignored him. "Jenny . . . do you understand what I'm saying? Can you tell us what happened to you?"

Still Jenny stared. She stared for so long that Malcolm glanced nervously at Wit and shook his head.

"Maybe she can't remember. Maybe she's in shock."

"What did you do?" Wit turned to him accusingly. "Kiss her goodnight?"

"You know," Jenny murmured, and Malcolm lowered his head to hear her.

"What did you say?"

54

"How could you . . . have done such a . . . terrible thing . . . to me." She closed her eyes wearily. "How could you?"

"I did something?" Malcolm sounded mystified. *"What* did I do?"

"Both of you . . . all of you."

"Jenny, listen to me." Malcolm leaned forward, his lips against her ear. "We found you at the bottom of the tower. At the foot of the stairs. Do you know—can you remember—how you got there?"

Jenny's eyes opened. She could feel her head shaking slowly, the pain threatening to explode.

"That can't be. You're lying. I was in that . . . room."

"What room?" Malcolm coaxed gently. "You'll have to explain it to me. I don't know what room you mean."

"You were there—someone *took* me there—"

"I was there?" Again Malcolm sounded bewildered. "Jenny, I haven't been anywhere with you. I came to check on you a little while ago, and that's when I found you by the stairs—"

"But you're *wrong!* I wasn't by the stairs, I was in that *room!"* Jenny's voice rose, and as she tried to sit up, Malcolm pushed her gently down again. "I *did* fall down the stairs, but that was *before!* There were noises in my room—rats, I'm *sure* of it—and that man with the hood and the rope—and I ran and *then* I fell! And someone picked me up and brought me to that *room!* And—you—all of you— were there in the dark—*don't lie to me!*—watching and laughing—saying those things to me—you

55

wanted to play that *game*—how *could* you—how could you do those horrible things to me and call it a game—"

Jenny's voice broke and she choked back a sob, fighting for control. She could see their faces above her, the way they glanced at each other with tight, strained faces, and she struggled to push Malcolm away.

"What . . . what things did you . . ." Malcolm took a deep breath, *"think* someone did to you?"

"Don't act like you don't know!" Jenny burst out, and Malcolm caught her hands and wrestled her carefully onto her pillow. "It was horrible, what you did—tying me up—that blindfold—dragging me across the floor and—"

"Sleepwalking," Wit interrupted, snapping his fingers. "Sleepwalking! In the tower! Very much like taking a long walk off a short pier!"

"Will you be quiet?" Malcolm shot him a dirty look and turned back to Jenny. He still had her hands trapped in his, and he was leaning across her, trying to keep her still. "You must have been dreaming, Jenny," he said quietly. "The whole thing sounds just too . . . too—" Watching tears well up in her eyes, he broke off and gave a long sigh. "You could have killed yourself falling. From now on I think we should bolt the door from the outside."

"No!" Jenny nearly screamed at him. "I didn't dream it, and I didn't imagine it! And I won't stay in this room! I want to talk to my father. Please— just take me to him now."

A quick, unreadable look passed between the two

boys. After a long moment Malcolm got up and moved toward the door.

"I'll . . . I'll be right back," he said, and Wit nodded, taking Malcolm's place upon the edge of the bed.

Jenny watched the door close and shifted her eyes to Wit's face.

"I didn't," she repeated stubbornly. "I didn't imagine it."

Wit was silent. He still wore his jester clothes, but not his cap, and his long reddish-brown hair curled loosely around his head. He reached into his pocket and withdrew three tiny balls, and as Jenny stared at him, he began to juggle them lazily into the air.

"All of us," he said, keeping his eyes on the balls. "All of us in some room doing terrible things to you."

Jenny sat up and hugged herself tightly. "Yes," she whispered.

"Your dad, too? Father?"

"No. Just you. You . . . three . . ." Jenny's voice trailed off in confusion.

"We three. Derreck and Malcolm and me."

Jenny said nothing. She wrapped her arms tighter around her chest, and Wit raised an eyebrow at her hesitation.

"You're positive," he said. "You saw us with your own eyes. You heard us with your own ears."

"Well . . ." A tear rolled down one of Jenny's cheeks, and she wiped it angrily away. "Not exactly . . ."

"I see. But before that, there were rats."

Jenny gave him a grudging nod. "Yes."

"Infesting your room. Hundreds of rats."

"Well . . . I thought so." She wiped another tear. "One or . . . or two, anyway."

Wit sighed, making the balls go higher. "And that's why you ran."

"That and the man."

"Ah, yes. The man with the hood. The ghost of Worthington Hall."

"Ghost?" Jenny looked shocked. "He wasn't a ghost. He was real."

"Really a ghost. *Realllly* scary."

The balls went higher. Wit grinned.

"He's an executioner, you know. He wanders the halls in the dead of night looking for victims to do in. You're not the first to see him."

"Ghost?" Jenny murmured. "But he had—"

"Sometimes an ax, sometimes a noose, nobody's safe when the hangman's loose."

"Then you've seen him, too?" Jenny leaned forward.

"No, of course I've never seen him. *I* happen to be an extremely rational and stable person." Wit shook his head condescendingly. "The *ghost,* you see, comes with the castle. What's a *castle* without it's own personal *ghost?*"

"I saw him," Jenny said stubbornly. "I wasn't asleep. I wasn't dreaming. I saw him."

Wit stretched out his hands and caught the balls, one by one.

"You asked about the family curse right before we left you tonight. Doesn't it make sense that it was the last thing on your mind before you went to sleep? And that you must have gone over it again in some weird nightmare?"

"It wasn't a nightmare," Jenny persisted. "I've had nightmares. Nothing ever like this."

"You took a pretty nasty fall. You've got bumps and bruises all over you. We know." He winked at her. "We checked."

In spite of herself Jenny blushed. She turned her head away from him and stared at the wall.

"An executioner," she mumbled. "A real one."

"A ghost."

"I don't believe in ghosts."

"Then you don't have anything to worry about."

"What else do you know about him?" Jenny chanced a quick look in Wit's direction and saw him smile.

"Oh, I get it. You *like* being terrified in your sleep, so you want me to help." Wit crossed his arms over his chest. "You really are a glutton for punishment."

"I want to know."

"Okay, let me think. I certainly wouldn't want to get any of this *wrong*—and have you ending up inside the *wrong* nightmare." He closed his eyes and furrowed his brow. *"They* said they saw him, too. The women who never survived here. Or at least"—his voice lowered conspiratorially—"that's what I've heard."

"What do you mean?"

"Every victim. Right before she met her untimely end. Every victim told about having seen the ghost."

"And no one believed them, either?"

Wit gave her a condescending look. "You *can't* prove anything when you're *dead.*"

"But you said they didn't all die."

"And what an incredible memory for detail you have. Well, unfortunately, *some* of them just lost their minds and lived on to speak of the ghost time and time again. Of course, *nobody* takes you seriously when you're crazy." He gave her a meaningful look. "I rest my case."

"Is this really the legend, or are you making this up?"

"It's all true," Wit said solemnly. "As true as your being in that room with me and Malcolm and Derreck doing horrible things to you."

"That's not funny."

"I'm not laughing."

"I think it really could have happened. And that you were all just trying to scare me. And this is part of the act."

"Right. You mustn't listen to me—after all, I'm only a fool."

"With a really sick sense of humor."

"Thank you." He bowed mockingly and slid the balls back into his pockets.

Jenny lay back and gazed up at the ceiling. She glanced at Wit and saw him glance just as quickly away.

"But how *could* it have been a dream?" she whispered again, unhappily. "How could it have been? . . ."

She shifted beneath the covers, then looked down at her legs in slow surprise.

"My nightgown," she said suddenly. "It's all wet. That has to mean *something,* doesn't it?"

"What? That this place leaks like a sieve? When Malcolm found you, you were lying in a puddle the size of a small swimming pool."

Jenny managed a slight nod . . . grew quiet. "So . . . there's no reason, is there? For you to believe me."

"It's magic, this house," Wit replied easily. He frowned and put one finger to his forehead as if pondering great thoughts. "Works on the mind. Twists it about. Makes you wonder. Makes you doubt." Jumping up from the bed, he spread his arms in an inclusive gesture. "Look around you. Is this not the stuff dreams are made of? *Evil* dreams, that is?"

"Then . . . if it didn't really happen . . ." Jenny's voice trailed off, too weary to finish.

"Who's to say dreams aren't real and reality's just a dream?" Wit gave her a mysterious smile. "It's been known to happen. Bumps on the head make for *straaaange* hallucinations. . . ."

"But you said I saw a ghost," Jenny mumbled. "You said the ghost was real."

Wit feigned surprise. "Did I? But you said you didn't believe. So which of us is right?"

He made a sudden turn and landed in the center of the room, so swiftly that Jenny hardly saw him move at all.

"But"—Jenny raised up on her elbows—"for just a second in that awful room . . . I really thought I saw Malcolm . . . or Derreck . . ."

"Then how would you tell them apart?" Wit finished her sentence triumphantly.

"And why would he—whoever he was—lie about being there? So if Malcolm says it wasn't him . . . then maybe it *was* Derreck."

"Or Malcolm disguised as Derreck," Wit added delightedly. "Or Derreck pretending to be Malcolm. I wouldn't know. *I* was in some other dream at the time, not yours." He twirled about and landed in the exact same position. "In dreams we see only bits and pieces. Thrown together"—he twirled again—"helter skelter without rhyme or reason. We need to put *all* the pieces together before we can have a pretty picture. Or"—his eyes narrowed—"sometimes the picture's not . . . so . . . pretty."

Jenny's head was throbbing. She made an impatient gesture and settled back down onto her pillow.

"I wish you'd just go. I wish you'd leave me alone."

"What you really wish is to know the difference between Malcolm and Derreck." Wit gave a sly grin and perched at the foot of her bed.

Again Jenny turned her face away and stared at the wall. "I don't care. I don't care anything about them."

She waited for him to answer, but he didn't. Silence settled thickly in the room, filling the space between them with a strange uneasiness. Without warning, Jenny felt a slow chill work its way up her spine. When Wit spoke at last, his teasing sounded almost forced.

"Perhaps you should," he said casually. "Just in

62

case you happen to meet one of them in a hallway after dark. Just in case one of them . . . creeps into your dreams."

Jenny turned and stared at him. "You sound almost as if . . . you believe me," she whispered.

Wit shook his head. "I didn't say that."

"But you . . . at least . . . think it's possible? That maybe I wasn't dreaming? Hallucinating? That something strange and horrible happened to me tonight?"

Wit crossed his legs, cocked his head, and began to rattle off, counting on his fingers:

"Derreck is quieter. Malcolm has more to say. Malcolm is the charming one; Derreck's more mysterious. They're exactly the same height, they have the same color hair and eyes, the same shaped face—though Derreck's is a *bit* thinner—the same arch to their brows. You can't tell them apart hearing them speak—though Derreck's voice *is* a trifle deeper. Same build, same weight, same bone structure. But . . ."

He scooted forward and rested the tip of one finger against his left earlobe.

"Perhaps it is that Derreck has a scar—just here. Beneath his hair, behind his ear? Small and . . . intimate, shall we say. Not so easy to find. You'd have to be quite . . . *close,*" he finished smugly.

Jenny watched him a moment, then frowned.

"None of that matters to me."

"Doesn't it?" And suddenly Wit's voice changed, the teasing completely gone, replaced by a note of seriousness. "There *is* a difference, Jenny—hear me and listen well. This is all I can tell."

He clamped his mouth shut as footsteps sounded on the stairs outside the door. Jenny shivered a little as Malcolm walked in.

"Where's my dad?" she asked, trying to peer around him. "Didn't you give him my message?"

Malcolm looked uncomfortable. He glanced at Wit but got no look in return.

"Well . . . the thing is, Jenny . . ."

"What?" And she could feel the fear building again, her body stiffening as she sat up, as Malcolm reached out to gently restrain her. "What are you talking about? Couldn't you find him? I want to see him now."

"You can't see him."

"Why not?"

"You just can't."

Again Malcolm looked at Wit. Wit looked at the floor and whistled softly under his breath.

"It's three in the morning, Jenny." Malcolm sighed. "We'd only been coming to check in on you—your dad told us not to tell you till morning."

"Tell me . . . what?"

"He got a call in the night. Some assignment he had to tend to right away."

"So . . . you're saying he's—"

"Gone." Malcolm nodded. "He's left you here with us till he comes back."

8

Jenny leaned over her plate and toyed listlessly with her breakfast. She hadn't slept a wink last night after Malcolm and Wit had left her room, and now she wondered how she'd ever be able to stay awake today. Wit had come for her early that morning and led her back to the main house, but she'd eaten alone. She was surprised when he suddenly appeared again, informing her she had a phone call in Sir John's study.

"Down there." Wit pointed her toward a corridor. "You look awful this morning, by the way."

"Well, at least I changed my clothes." Jenny retorted. "What do you do—sleep in that costume?"

Wit struck a pose. "We're all at the fair on display—we run back and forth all the day—doing well at our jobs, entertaining the mobs—so we must live the parts that we play!"

Jenny glowered at him before turning her back. She didn't expect the study to be occupied, so she was surprised when she heard voices inside. Pressing against the wall, she put her ear close to the open door and listened.

"Of course it's inconvenient," Sir John hissed. "What do you *think?*"

"I think we should get her out of here," a familiar voice replied. *Malcolm? Or Derreck?* "In fact, I think she should never have come at all."

"Granted, but it's done now, isn't it? And I can't very well turn her out. We mustn't do *anything* to arouse suspicion. Everything must go on as normal as possible. I *need* the publicity—to bring the *tourists*—to spend the *money*—to keep this *house!*" Sir John's voice rose. "Dammit, just her being here is—"

"Dangerous," the other finished.

"More than dangerous," Sir John muttered. "Tragic at the very least."

"Well, then, perhaps you haven't considered the very worst."

Sir John sounded angry. "So now at last you're beginning to understand the magnitude of our predicament—"

"Not our. *Yours.* You already know how *we* all feel about it."

There was a moment of silence. Even from her hiding place, Jenny could feel the tension in the air.

"This must be *your* responsibility," Sir John said coldly. "I can't do it alone. It's up to you three to take care of her."

"Really? Easier said than done, I should think, considering the circumstances."

"I'm sure you'll think of something."

"I'm sure we'll have to."

Footsteps moved rapidly through the room. Jenny had only a split second to squeeze herself behind the doors before one of the twins strode out and disappeared down the corridor. In less than a minute Sir John also came out and walked off in the opposite direction as Jenny slipped quietly into the study and picked up the telephone.

Her father didn't even wait for her to say hello.

"Jenny, it's an important assignment," Mr. Logan greeted her. "I'm the only one who can cover it—I don't have a choice, I *have* to do it! And with your mother galavanting off to Paris—"

"She's not galavanting!" Jenny's voice rose. "She's away on business and—"

"Whatever. The point is, I promised her I'd keep you, so you'll have to stay there till I get back."

"I can't." Jenny gripped the phone so tightly that her knuckles hurt. "Dad, I *can't* stay here! Something happened last night—is happening—right now—"

"Yes, yes, Sir John told me—some silly nightmare. I wish you wouldn't upset everyone with that imagination of yours, Jenny—remember you're a guest!"

"But, Dad—"

"Look, I'm sorry I ran out on you, but I had a plane to catch, and there was no point in waking you up. It'll only be for a couple days. In the meantime I want you to take over for me there. Get some pictures or something. Human interest stuff."

"All I've got is my little camera! How can I take pictures for you? Dad, about last night—"

"Make notes, then. Ask questions. Jot down your impressions of the castle and the fair and all the people you meet. My next interview's the first of next week—I *can't* miss it. So you'll have to do most of the research for me. Understand? I don't know how long it'll take to get the damn car fixed—we'll just have to rent one till I can get back there to pick mine up. Maybe I can get some money from your mother or . . . well, never mind about that. I'll see you day after tomorrow. I'll only have *one* day to spend when I get there—and I can see now that's going to mean one whole day of shooting photos—so I'm counting on you to have all the other research done for me. Sir John said he'd love to have you."

Jenny heard his voice through a layer of numbness. Her gaze wandered around Sir John's huge chamber, then settled back on the window, where the morning shone through, bright and fresh and clean after the rain.

"Jenny?" Dad's voice brought her back. "Did you hear me?"

"I heard."

"Okay, then. Do a good story for me, kid."

There was a click and a dial tone. Jenny hung up and leaned against the table, feeling sick.

"You're missing the fair," a voice spoke behind her, and she turned to see one of the twins in the doorway.

"Oh, you scared me—" Jenny straightened up and stared at him. "Malcolm?"

A slow smile went over his lips. He shook his head, then disappeared.

For a long time Jenny stood gazing after him, then she gave a deep sigh and turned again to the window. Far below to her left she could see a curve of rocky shoreline, water lapping and foaming along the cliffs at its edge. In the opposite direction an overgrown field stretched nearly half a mile before it began a gentle slope downward and out of sight. The sky was brilliantly blue, and in the distance colorful banners snapped in the wind, just visible in the partially hidden valley below. *That must be the fair going on down there. . . .*

"So. How *is* your father this morning."

Jenny started as Sir John came up behind her and laid one hand upon her shoulder. His touch was as cold as ice.

"Busy," she murmured.

"Yes. The sad fate of journalists, I suppose." The old man gave a slow smile, and Jenny realized how much he must have resembled the twins in his younger days. "As I promised your father, I'll be more than happy to be of any assistance I can. And that, of course, extends to my boys."

"Is that the fair down there?" Jenny changed the subject.

Sir John moved close to her, narrowing his eyes on the windowpane.

"At the bottom of the hill, yes. I think you'll find it most amusing, Jenny, and especially today. This is Visitors' Costume Day—most of the tourists will be dressed in period clothes. Prizes for the best, and so forth. I'm sure I could find you something to wear if—"

"No, thank you."

He regarded her thoughtfully. "It's a phenomenon, really. The way participants seem to forget about this modern century once they pass through the gates. A sort of magic. Stepping back in time."

"Has it started yet?"

"Of course. The fair opens early and won't close until dusk. Here. Use this free pass. With my compliments."

He turned to go, but Jenny's voice stopped him.

"Sir John—now that my father's gone, do you think I could use his room?"

The old man seemed to be thinking. After a long pause he turned back to face her.

"I'm so sorry, my dear." He shook his head. "And especially after that grisly nightmare of yours my sons told me about. The truth of the matter is, last night's storm seems to have severely damaged one of the windows in there. I'm afraid that room is completely out of the question."

Jenny stood stiffly, watching as another smile crept across his lips.

"You will enjoy yourself"—he nodded slightly —"won't you?"

He didn't wait for Jenny to answer. He went off again down the hall, and Jenny watched from the doorway to make sure he'd really gone.

It was already hot when she got outside. Last night's rain had left the air thick with humidity, and by the time she neared the foot of the hill, she was out of breath. Her mind felt dull from lack of sleep, and she couldn't stop the discussion she'd just overheard from playing over and over in her brain—*"Dangerous . . . Tragic . . . It's up to you three to take care of her . . ."*

Who were they talking about? Me?

She stopped, an icy chill crawling over her in spite of the heat.

But why? What reason would they possibly have for talking about me?

"Let's scare Jenny to death. . . ."

"Oh, God . . ."

Jenny closed her eyes and tilted her face up to the sun. Warmth spread across her cheeks, and she willed it into the dark, confused corners of her mind.

I didn't hear them say my name in the study. They could have been talking about anyone, anyone at all. I'm just overreacting—being paranoid. Dad's right—I do have an overactive imagination. It's because of that dream last night—and it must have been a dream—it had to be a dream—nothing real could be that horrible—no real person could ever be that cruel. . . .

She tried to conjure up the voices once more from the study, tried to concentrate on what she'd overheard, but nothing made any sense to her. Nothing at all.

"We mustn't do anything to arouse suspicion. . . ."

Jenny started walking. She lifted one hand, wincing as she touched the bump on her head. If Dad were here, he'd tell her not to jump to conclusions.

He'd tell her not to assume anything without examining the cold, hard facts.

This crack on my head . . . that's a hard fact, she thought ruefully. *And these cuts and bruises on my arms and legs—those are more facts. Falling down the stairs . . . eavesdropping outside a door where I shouldn't have been in the first place . . . where I probably missed out on the main part of the conversation that wasn't even my business . . .*

Jenny sighed and walked faster. Without Dad here, she *wanted* to believe that everything was all right. That Sir John was just an odd, eccentric old man. That Derreck and Malcolm and Wit were just impossible pranksters. That last night's terrors had only been a dream.

She *needed* to believe it. Needed to . . . with all her heart.

She squared her shoulders and continued on down the hill.

To Jenny's surprise a huge crowd had already gathered, milling about in front of the gates. She saw the false front of a castle rising tall into the sky, the guards posted on either side of the entrance, the fluttering banners, the high encircling walls with rooftops and bright colors showing beyond. There was a festive feeling of excitement as people streamed by, and she stared in amazement at the lines and lines of medieval characters, their clothing strangely out of context with the rows of cars parked in the surrounding fields.

Research, huh? Jenny frowned, remembering her father's orders. *Well, I might as well see what there is to see—there's nothing else to do around here anyway.* Handing over her pass, Jenny joined the eager mob and went in to the fair.

She'd never seen anything like it in her life.

As if the simple act of walking beneath the arched entrance had magically transported her centuries backward, from one world to another.

Everywhere, in any direction she looked, there was something going on—minstrels singing, costumed street characters greeting one another, vendors selling food, craftspeople at their trades, demonstrations of physical prowess and skill, musicians playing instruments, acrobats, mimes, lords and ladies parading with their retinues. Jenny could scarcely take it all in, it was so real, so convincing. Wandering through the lazily twisting maze of pathways, she soon realized that the fair was set up as a series of large open clearings connected by wide avenues of sawdust-covered earth, overhung and enclosed by a natural landscape of thick, lush trees. There were authentic shops, huts, and theaters; footbridges over gurgling creeks; tents and carts; even a petting zoo with baby animals. As she came upon a food area, such delicious aromas wafted over her that her stomach growled, and she remembered she hadn't really eaten much of her breakfast. She walked slowly around the enclosure, trying to decide what to get—everything from meat pies to dried fruits, apple cider to ale, scones to pizza—and finally decided on a roasted turkey leg hot off the grill.

Munching her snack, Jenny went on, smiling as people greeted her, getting totally caught up in the friendly atmosphere. She passed a falconer with his falcons, hawks, and eagles, then paused to laugh at a puppet show. She watched as apples were squeezed in a cider press, as the art of blacksmithing was demonstrated, as two competitors tried to outwit each other in an ongoing game of chess. She was just dodging two children with stick horses when someone grabbed her from behind, and she spun around, nearly dropping her food.

"Black and blue becomes you." Wit winked at her. Then, with a mischievous look, he shouted, "Nice to see you in your clothes for a change!"

Jenny's cheeks flamed. As people turned to look at her, she took off in the opposite direction, with Wit close at her heels.

"Should I have explained?" He tried to look forlorn. "Should I have said something about your nightgown or—"

"Just don't say anything. Go away."

"Uh-oh."

"What?"

"Quick—close your eyes!"

"What?" Jenny stopped, alarmed. "What about my—"

"Don't talk! Just hurry—close your eyes right now—there's something—"

"Something what?"

"Just do it!"

Jenny did as she was told, shutting her eyes tight as Wit stepped up to her.

"Something on your eyelashes," he whispered. "Oh, no—I knew it—oh, no—something on your . . ."

As Jenny stood stock still, she felt the slightest pressure on one eyelid, and she held her breath.

"What is it?" she murmured.

"A kiss."

For one startled moment she couldn't even open her eyes. When she finally did, Wit's nose was touching hers, and he was smiling.

"It's all right," he said. "I took care of it."

Another blush crept over Jenny's face. She didn't know whether to laugh or be furious with him.

"Don't hit me," Wit whispered. "I wound easily."

At that Jenny couldn't help but smile, and as he stepped back from her, she studied him closely in the sunlight.

He was exactly her height, with a slight, slender build, and a dimple showing in one cheek. There was a naughty twinkle in his blue eyes as though he were up to something delightfully wicked, and when he began walking again, she noticed a spring to his step, as if he were not only weightless but without a care in the world.

"Cute," Jenny said, hiding a smile. "Has anyone ever told you how cute you are?"

"I am, indeed, there's no one in the world as cute or clever as me." Wit beamed. "I'm the best at being cute, but I never get the girl."

Jenny laughed. "She'd have to be a fool to fall in love with you."

"Very *good!* I'm *impressed!*" Wit chuckled. "Have you been through the whole fair by now?"

"No, not all of it."

"Then come with me. There's more to see!"

Jenny could hardly keep up with him, he moved so quickly through the crowds. Along the way he managed to pull at least a dozen girls' hair, engage in a pantomime swordfight with a little boy, pluck three apples from a cart, which he promptly began to juggle before the vendor caught him, and slyly hug a blushing old woman behind her husband's back. Jenny was laughing so hard by the time they stopped again, it took her a few minutes to notice where they were.

"Gypsy camp," Wit announced, pushing her forward into yet another clearing. "See anyone you recognize?"

Jenny could hear violins and tambourines and the shouts of dancers as the crowd clapped in time. Stepping closer to one of the wagons, she saw a tall young man with his head bent back, swallowing a spear of fire. The crowd gasped and began to applaud, and as the gypsy straightened up, he looked right at Jenny with his dark, piercing eyes.

It was one of the twins.

"The girls love him," Wit whispered, "because he's so *hot.*"

Jenny elbowed Wit in the stomach. "Is that Derreck?"

"For my next event," the gypsy called out, motioning the crowd closer, "I shall need a volunteer."

His voice was deep and seductive, yet he didn't seem to notice the effect he was having on the girls in the audience. As Jenny looked around, every female seemed totally mesmerized.

"Me! Me!" In a high-pitched voice Wit began yelling, and before Jenny even realized what he was doing, he grabbed her arm and waved it high in the air. "Pick me! I think you're gorgeous!"

"Stop that!" she hissed at him, but the crowd was laughing now, and as the gypsy focused in on the sound of Wit's voice, she saw the recognition on his handsome face, the slow smile on his lips.

"By all means, help the lady up," he said.

"No—oh, please—I don't want to!" Frantically Jenny tried to escape, but Wit pushed her firmly to the stage and up the steps.

"She's a little shy," Wit said apologetically, and again the crowd laughed as the gypsy reached out and grasped Jenny firmly by the hand.

"No need to be," the gypsy said smoothly. "We're all friends here."

Jenny spun around to give Wit a murderous look, but he'd completely vanished. Shocked, she looked every which way through the crowd, but the gypsy was pulling her, guiding her to the other end of the platform.

"What—what are you doing?" Jenny asked, conscious now of a wall behind her, conscious now of his hands upon her—touching her shoulders, her arms, her head—placing her in position, just so . . .

"Don't move," he said softly. Untying the wide red sash from around his waist, he looped it around Jenny's, then fastened the ends to a ring on the wall.

"What? Derreck? Wait—what are you—"

"Don't move."

Totally mystified, Jenny stayed where he placed her, watching as he walked off and began to reach into a wooden box. She heard the low murmuring of the crowd, the undercurrent of nervousness as they looked at one another, as they looked from the mysterious gypsy—to her—then back again—

And as he raised his arms above his head, Jenny saw the silver blades glinting in the sunlight, the long gleaming daggers clutched tightly in his hands.

9

Jenny couldn't move.

As she realized what was going to happen, every muscle locked, and her feet froze to the stage.

"Razor sharp," the gypsy announced, holding the knives where the crowd could see. A thrill of uneasiness stirred through the onlookers. They jostled each other and shifted their gazes back to Jenny.

"Razor sharp." He said it again, mechanically and without emotion, as if he'd given the same speech over and over many times. "One slip could prove . . . uncomfortable, at the very least. Fatal . . . at the very worst."

Jenny stared, her mouth open. She could see the gypsy's dark, dark stare, the red scarf around his head, the gold earring in his ear. She could see the muscles tensing in his cheek as he measured her

79

slowly with his eyes. And suddenly she could hear the voice again, in the study just hours ago, one of the twins—*"Perhaps you haven't considered the very worst. . . ."*

Malcolm? Derreck?

Something cold pounded in Jenny's head. A trickle of sweat slid down her forehead, but she was afraid to brush it off.

"I must have total silence," the gypsy went on. "Total concentration. It would be a pity to . . . mar . . . such a beautiful face."

Jenny swallowed, her mouth dry as cotton.

"Look at me," the gypsy ordered her.

His eyes narrowed upon her face. She felt the fathomless intensity of his gaze, and suddenly everything else seemed to fade away—to disappear—and there was only him, him and nobody else, drawing her to him, pulling her in . . .

Jenny saw the tight line of his lips, the angle of his jaw; she saw something flicker deep in his stare as he aimed the first dagger.

No . . . stop . . .

There wasn't even time to close her eyes.

Something landed with a thud beside her head, and she choked on a scream.

"Stop!" she tried to shout at him, but her throat was closing up, she couldn't breathe, and as she focused in on him through a haze of fear, she saw him poise the next dagger.

She felt as if she was going to collapse.

"Don't move," he said curtly, and she *was* going to faint, she knew it, all those people staring, watching her, the gypsy's dark eyes pinning her to the wall—

"No—don't—"

She never saw the blade hit, only felt the sudden slice across the side of her neck, heard the crowd screaming, saw the calm, detached look on the gypsy's face. And there was blood trickling down her sleeve, and people running toward the stage, and she was swooning . . . falling . . . blood on her neck, her shoulder, dripping onto her shirt . . .

As if from a great distance she saw the gypsy standing over her.

He made no move to help. Only stared.

"I'd say you need more practice." Wit suddenly appeared from nowhere, pushing his brother out of the way. He caught Jenny as she slumped against the wall, and with one quick movement he jerked the sash from around her. "Do something with these people—I'll get her inside."

Wit steered her to the closest wagon. As he sat her in a chair, Jenny glanced around the cluttered interior and saw an assortment of costumes, take-out-food containers, musical instruments, and cardboard props. She reached dazedly for her neck and jumped as she touched Wit's fingers instead.

"What are you doing?" Instantly she recoiled, looking down with dismay at the blood on her hand.

"Saving your neck," Wit retorted. "Or put more simply, keeping you from bleeding to death."

"Bleeding to—" Again her hand went to her neck, but Wit grabbed it and pushed it firmly away.

"Do you mind?"

"How bad is it?" Jenny asked weakly.

"You look pale. You're not going to do the fainting thing on me, are you?"

Jenny managed to shake her head. "I can't believe it. I can't believe this is happening. He practically decapitated me, and he didn't even look sorry."

"Derreck?" Wit mumbled, pressing a cloth against her neck. "Or Malcolm? On the contrary, I've *always* thought he's pretty sorry-looking."

Jenny started an angry reply to his teasing but he forced her head down. Gazing at the floor, she was surprised to see two bare feet and a long skirt appear behind him in the open doorway.

"Poor girl," someone whispered. "Poor, poor girl—"

Wit released Jenny so quickly that she almost fell from the chair. Catching herself, she turned toward the door and saw Wit facing the same direction.

"Nan." He lifted one eyebrow, an expression between disgust and amusement. "How charming you look. As always."

With a start, Jenny realized who it was. The girl's hair was still dirty and tangled; she was still wearing the torn, sloppy dress. And as her wild dark eyes gazed back at Jenny, they looked every bit as frightened as they had last night at the gatehouse.

"Blood," she whispered, moving slowly into the room. "More blood, just like I knew. I'm always right. I try to say, but people don't listen—"

"Don't listen? Imagine that," Wit broke in. "And you such a *stimulating* conversationalist."

"They'd go," she insisted. "All of you and everyone—they'd all go if they knew—they'd all—"

"But you're the one who should go," a deep voice said, and without warning, one of the twins materialized on the threshold. "It's time for you to dance, isn't it, Nan?" he added evenly.

Nan whirled around, her face pale, but it was Jenny who spoke first.

"Look what you did!" she burst out angrily. "You could have scarred me for life!"

Beside her, Nan stiffened and locked eyes with the gypsy, then slowly turned back, her eyes now full on Jenny. As Jenny met her gaze, she thought there might have been a flicker of recognition in the girl's eyes, but it vanished almost immediately.

"I don't believe you've met our guest, have you, Nan," Wit said, busy with Jenny's wound again. "This is Jenny."

"No," Nan murmured, swaying gently from side to side, hugging herself. "No . . . I don't believe I have."

"But I *have* met you before, Nan," Jenny spoke up. "Don't you remember? Last night when my dad and I were driving in—you were—"

Jenny broke off, staring hard at the girl. There was absolutely no acknowledgment in Nan's expression; she was simply staring off into space. Uneasily Jenny let the subject drop and realized for the first time that both boys were watching her, their faces curious and unsmiling. And suddenly Jenny was aware of something else—something nagging at the back of her mind, far back where she couldn't quite grasp it—*something . . . but what?*

"Go on, Nan," the gypsy's voice was flat. "They're all waiting for you."

"For . . . for me?" A tremulous smile came to the girl's lips, and he nodded.

"Of course. For you."

As Nan slipped out, the gypsy moved over to stand beside Wit. Feeling his eyes upon her, Jenny stared at him indignantly, surprised when Wit spoke for her.

"Next time you try piercing her ears," Wit said dryly, "aim a bit higher, won't you?"

"I didn't throw it," his brother said, and Wit's head came up, eyes narrowing in on the other's face. The gypsy shook his head slowly, and after a slight hesitation, Wit looked down once more.

"You tried to cut my head off"—Jenny's voice shook—"and I saw you with the knife in your hand, so don't say—"

"I didn't throw it," the gypsy repeated calmly. "And, by the way, I find your lovely head much more attractive right here on your shoulders." He ran his fingertips lightly along her neck, smiling when Jenny shivered. "Just a scratch. It's not even bleeding anymore."

"You threw it at me and you missed!" she insisted, pulling away from him. "Why can't you just admit it?"

"I never miss," he said.

Jenny looked at Wit. The jester's brow was furrowed in thought, but though he stared back at her, then up at his brother, he said nothing.

"S-so—" Jenny stammered, "what you're trying to tell me is—what *are* you trying to tell me?"

Wit lowered his eyes. The gypsy shrugged.

"It happens sometimes. Someone in the crowd gets a little overzealous. Drunk, maybe. Too caught up in the make-believe."

"Make-believe!" Jenny exclaimed. "This is *real!*"

"Careful . . . careful . . ." Wit warned. "Don't make your blood boil—it'll all run out your neck!"

Jenny grabbed the cloth from him and flung it to the floor. "I don't believe this! A knife flies straight at my head out of nowhere, and you call it make-believe? And while we're at it, this stupid guessing-the-twin game isn't funny—it's rude! Who *are* you anyway"—she pointed at the gypsy—"Derreck or Malcolm?"

To Jenny's fury, his face went blank. "Let me think . . ." he said slowly. "It's so hard to tell us apart . . ."

Wit snatched up the cloth again and regarded the bloodstains in mock horror. "There was a young girl at the fair, who dodged a sharp knife in thin air! When she tried to find out what the fuss was about, everyone that she asked said 'Beware!'"

Jenny turned on him, pointing to her neck. "This isn't a joke."

"No," Wit said solemnly, "you're absolutely right. It's a neck. Now, if you'll just hold still so I can put a bandage on—"

"Oh, wait, I get it—I dreamed it, right?" Jenny stood up and glared at them. "Maybe last night, but it's daylight now. Or—or—maybe I did it myself!

Just a little trick thing I came up with, because I like pain—"

"I'm a pain." Wit winked at her. "Do you like me?"

"I can't believe you two." Jenny shook her head in amazement. "If it happened to me, it could happen to anyone else out there. Aren't you at least going to report it or something? Warn people?"

Slowly Wit straightened up. Jenny saw his eyes meet his brother's, and she could swear some silent exchange of messages had taken place.

"Whoever did it probably panicked and ran." The gypsy crossed his arms over his chest and leaned back against the wall. "I doubt he'll ever be back here again. Why panic everyone else?"

"Because maybe he didn't leave," Jenny retorted. "Because maybe he's still lurking around somewhere."

"Then maybe it *was* you." Wit raised an eyebrow at the gypsy. "You're good at lurking."

"Or maybe it was *you,*" his brother said smoothly. "Where were *you* when it happened?"

"Oh, that's right, blame the jester!" Wit flung his hands into the air. "Always blame the jester when the least little thing goes wrong! A crazed jester loose at the fair, targeting innocent young girls!" He sidled up to Jenny and lowered his voice suggestively. "You are . . . *innocent* . . . aren't you?"

Jenny was fuming. As she looked from one to the other, she shoved out fiercely at Wit. The jester spun in exaggerated circles, smashed himself loudly against the wall, and crumpled to the floor in a heap.

"What?" he groaned pathetically. "Was it something I said?"

The gypsy watched the performance a moment, then went over to help Wit up. As Wit got on his feet once more, the gypsy looked back at Jenny, his expression bland.

"You won't go spreading rumors, will you," he said quietly. "You seem like such a sensible girl."

He glanced at Wit, who nodded in agreement. The jester cocked his head and wagged a finger at Jenny's face.

"Why, the next thing you know," he scolded, "you'll believe someone's trying to kill you."

10

Jenny was glad to be out in the sun again. As she stormed away from the wagon, she took huge gulps of air and tried not to cry. Her neck hurt, and she was still shaking. *How can they be so insensitive—like nothing happened! That stupid game of twins—not being able to tell one from the other—*She could still see the knives in the gypsy's hands . . . could still see the look in his eyes as he'd prepared to throw . . . *It must have been Derreck—but why would he want to hurt me?*

She was almost past another wagon when the gypsy music stopped her. Joining the crowd gathered there, she could see Nan dancing up onstage, her eyes closed, her body moving gracefully. As Jenny stood and stared, the girl's eyes opened and settled on her face, and for one weird second it was as if Nan had become oblivious to the music, the people, everything except Jenny's presence. Uneasily Jenny backed away, relieved when Nan resumed her dancing.

Jenny hurried toward the main gates, amazed at how the crowds had grown. The narrow streets were packed so tightly with people now, it was hard to walk, and with relief she spotted a side path leading off through some woods behind a row of shops. Hoping it might be a shortcut, Jenny swung off the main thoroughfare and headed into the trees.

Quiet enveloped her almost at once. As Jenny ventured farther from the fairgrounds, she found herself entirely surrounded by lush, low-sweeping branches, deep carpets of pine needles, and sloping banks of ivy. Mist hung in the air from last night's rain, curling up like steam from the wet places below, muting the songs of the birds, swirling the scenery in hazy shades of green. With a deep sigh Jenny stopped and put one hand to her head. She had to sit down for a minute. She had to think.

Spying a fallen log near the top of a low rise, she managed the climb easily and settled herself in the grass. A warm breeze fanned her cheeks, and she bent her head back, gently fingering the line of dried blood along her neck. At least the gypsy— whoever he was—had been right about one thing —it didn't seem to be too deep. She trailed one hand over her cheek and shuddered. What if it had sliced right through the side of her face instead? Or lodged straight into her throat? *Which means whoever threw it was either extremely lucky or an extremely good aim. . . .*

Frowning, Jenny leaned her head back and rested

it against the log. *Good aim* . . . She remembered her horrible dream of last night . . . *Dream? I could have been killed so easily* . . . and then the knife missing her face this morning by only a fraction of an inch. *I could have been killed, but I wasn't—why?*

She shut her eyes and groaned softly. What was it Wit had told her? *"The next thing you know, you'll believe someone's trying to kill you. . . ."*

A restless wind sighed through the trees. Jenny kept her eyes closed and let herself drift. She could smell rich, damp earth and crushed leaves and wildflowers. . . . She could hear the faint patter of wings, the hum of bees, the faraway caw of a crow. *I don't want to go back to the castle. . . . I want to stay here, where it's peaceful, where it's safe—*

Jenny bolted upright, her heart pounding.

"What?" she shouted. "Who's there?"

The forest stretched deep and dreamlike around her. She scooted back against the log and drew her knees up to her chest.

I heard something—I swear I did—I heard someone call my name—

Jenny listened, every muscle tense. There were no woodland sounds to comfort her now—the birds had gone suddenly still. Straining her ears, she let her gaze travel slowly along the rise . . . down the slope . . . around the circle of encroaching trees . . . It seemed darker to her now . . . darker than it had only moments before. *Did I fall asleep? How long have I been out?*

"Hello?" Jenny whispered. "Is anyone there?"

A breath of air crept over her shoulders, raising

the hair at the back of her neck. Jenny got to her feet and waited. After several long minutes she took a cautious step to the edge of the slope and looked down into the heavy mist.

Even when he came toward her, she couldn't believe it.

Even when he pulled slowly from the shadows beneath the trees and stood watching her, she stayed on the hillside and gazed at him through a numbness of disbelief.

She saw the hood that covered his head . . .

And the coil of rope in his black-gloved hands . . .

And as he waited for her to make a move, she could see the way he twisted the noose back and forth . . . back and forth . . . so calmly . . .

"No," Jenny gasped. "No!"

As she crashed blindly through the trees, she could hear branches snapping behind her, the ground thudding beneath his boots as he swiftly closed the distance between them. She didn't know where she was going, where she could run, her only hope to somehow find her way back to the fair. Spotting a low break in the foliage ahead, Jenny veered sharply and flung herself to the ground, scrambling on hands and knees into a thicket of clotted shrubs and vines. Several feet into her hiding place, she flattened herself against the ground and lay there motionless, praying for him to go by.

She could feel the vibrations beneath her cheek. She could feel him getting closer.

She closed her eyes, terrified even to breathe.

She knew the exact second he stopped.

The exact second he waited, listening for her to make a mistake . . .

Somehow she knew he would wait forever . . . no matter how long it might take.

Jenny lost all track of time. As she kept herself molded tightly to the ground, she couldn't feel her muscles anymore, and her thoughts began to float crazily in all directions. She thought she might have dozed once or twice—she couldn't be sure. She knew it was getting darker, that fog was settling over her. . . . She had a vague realization that once night fell, she'd never find her way back to the house. *He must still be out there—I never heard him go away. . . .*

Something touched her foot.

As Jenny shrieked in terror, she kicked out and tried to twist around. She caught just a glimpse of the raccoon as it bounded off through the underbrush, chattering at her angrily.

Jenny sat there and stared. At any second she expected a gloved hand to reach out of the darkness and snatch her away. . . .

A gloved hand . . .

And suddenly she knew what had been bothering her back there in the wagon when she'd met Nan—what had been nagging at her from some corner of memory . . .

The gloved hand.

She remembered now driving in with Dad last night—the guard at the gatehouse, and the way he'd kept out of reach of the light. She hadn't been able to see his body . . . just black shadows and a gloved hand reaching out of the darkness. She hadn't been able to see his head or his face . . . *just a cold gleam of eyes . . . looking out at her from a hood. . . .*

A convulsion of fear shook Jenny to the bone.

The executioner . . .

The ghost of Worthington Hall . . .

"Then . . . is he real?"

The sound of her voice frightened her; Jenny didn't realize she'd spoken out loud. If he was anywhere near her now, he surely would have heard, alerted before by her careless scream. . . .

But nothing happened.

It took her a long while to believe she was really safe. A long while to work up the courage to crawl out again and stand on her shaky legs, to survey her surroundings and coax her mind into functioning. Twilight had already smudged the woods with deep, secret pockets of darkness. She had no idea which way to go.

But it doesn't mean anything, she argued silently to herself, *it doesn't mean anything, not really. Dreams are funny, like Wit said, bits and pieces of things thrown together. I saw something when we drove here, and then I could have planted it somehow in my nightmare. It could have just taken on the form of an executioner because I was in the castle and thinking of castle things and Wit told me about the family curse and it could all have gotten jumbled up together—it doesn't mean anything at all. I'm doing it again—making things up to scare myself, as if I weren't scared enough already—*

In spite of her frenzied reasoning, Jenny didn't

feel any better. She started walking, her body sluggish and mechanical. *I can't be that far away from the castle. . . . It couldn't be that hard to find.* She remembered last night and how Worthington Hall had loomed up so suddenly from the darkness, and she told herself it would be the same way now, that just around the next stand of trees she'd see its tall menacing towers holding up the sky. . . .

Yet it wasn't the castle that waited for her around the next grove of trees . . . not the castle that stopped her in her tracks and sent her scurrying back into cover of shadows so she could listen without being seen.

The voices were low and urgent. There were several of them, and they sounded as if they were arguing. Jenny tried to make them out, but she was too far away to hear plainly, only snatches of conversation as tempers and emotions seemed to flare.

"You've *got* to do it. Do you hear? Look at me!"

A male voice. Tight with barely controlled fury. There was a soft scuttle, and then sharp gasps, as if someone were being shaken. Alarmed, Jenny heard the sound of crying. *A girl?*

"You know what'll happen if you don't." The boy spoke again. *Malcolm? Derreck?* "You know we're *all* in danger. Every one of us."

"I—I—can't. He won't like it—"

Nan?

"Won't like it! Who the hell cares what he likes! Today could have been a *disaster!* Not to mention last night! Do you even realize how close—"

"It wasn't my fault!"

94

"Look . . . don't cry. . . . What we're trying to say is, you can't treat this like something normal anymore." Another voice this time. Softer. Kinder. *Wit?* "It's *not* normal, understand? This sort of thing . . . it's—"

"I'm warning you," the first voice broke in, seething. "We're *all* warning you. It's got to be done soon. And keep . . . your . . . mouth . . . *shut.* If I find out you've tried to help him—"

"Leave her alone! Threatening her won't do any good—she doesn't understand—" And there was *fear* in this voice, Jenny could actually *feel* the fear—feel its *panic. But the same voice or a different one? I can't tell—*

"She better understand. She better damn well under—"

Abruptly the voices stopped.

As Jenny cowered there in the darkness, she distinctly heard the sound of hinges groaning— *Hinges? out here in the woods?*—and after that, something being thrown to the ground.

For an endless moment there was only silence.

And then the sobs came . . . deep . . . and empty . . . and hopeless.

11

Jenny had never heard such pitiful sounds.

She closed her eyes and fought back tears of her own as she tried to decide what to do. Step out and reveal herself? Or wait awhile longer, just to make sure the voices had really gone?

Dusk had turned to darkness. Around her the fog thickened and swirled through the trees—sad, lost spirits beckoning Jenny closer. Taking a deep breath, she stepped from her hiding place and put her hands to her mouth, calling softly into the night.

"Nan? Nan, is that you?"

There was a quick intake of breath—a choked scream.

"No, Nan, wait!"

In despair Jenny heard the light footsteps running away, disappearing into the woods. *She probably thought I was a ghost—no wonder she ran. . . .*

Now there were no sounds at all. As if the fog had sucked everything in . . . swallowed it whole. Through a break in the distant trees Jenny could see pale moonlight filtering down, and she groped her way carefully to where she thought the voices might have been.

Hinges . . . am I going crazy? I know I heard them. . . .

She stopped and squinted through the gloom. She was fairly certain the voices had come from this particular area, but though she turned in a slow circle, all she saw were trees, heavily knotted underbrush, and scraggy ledges covered with mats of trailing vines. Ahead of her the forest yawned blackly, and as she groaned in frustration, she sagged back and rested her head against the rock.

Only it wasn't rock.

Startled, Jenny whirled around and ran her hands over the face of the ledge. Beneath the ivy she could feel the roughness of wood, and moving farther down, she discovered a small handle completely concealed by thick leaves.

Jenny held her breath.

Are they right on the other side of the door— waiting for me to open it—to go in—another trick —another joke—

Her pulse pounded in her temples.

She pushed on the door, and once again the groan of rusty hinges echoed through the woods.

Jenny froze and waited.

Nothing happened.

Slowly she stepped inside and pulled the door shut behind her.

To her surprise, she found herself in a narrow, arched tunnelway, its ceiling so low she had to bend down to walk. Stubs of candles flickered from niches in the slimy walls—some of them already burnt out—and Jenny went as quickly as she could while there was still enough light to see by. *They must have gone this way—the voices I heard—this must lead back to the house. . . .*

As the tunnel wound on and on, Jenny began to be aware of a strange unpleasant odor, faint at first, then stronger, as if some foul draft had begun seeping along the passage. She quickened her pace and glanced back over her shoulder into the throbbing shadows behind. She was certain the smell hadn't been there when she'd first come in, but now the tunnel seemed to be closing up around her, dank air pressing from all sides. Like something dead, she thought uneasily, *like something rotten. . . .*

Jenny moved faster and tried not to think at all. Better to blank out her mind, better to concentrate on putting one foot in front of the other. *This tunnel can't go on forever . . . I've got to end up somewhere. But where?* Dark images crowded into her mind, and she fought to push them away. *Voices in the woods . . . bloody knives . . . running through the fog . . . that hooded man—I didn't dream it—I couldn't have dreamed it—and why did Nan act like she didn't know me? Why does she act so strange, so scared?*

And *she* was running now, running through the cramped tunnel, running from the fears and the questions, and the smell was stronger now—unbearable—*death*—*decay*—filling her head, suffocating her so that she couldn't breathe, so that she stumbled and fell against the wall, screaming as it gave way beneath her, as it swung inward and spilled her upon the ground. . . .

She lay there a moment, blinking into the dim, dim light. She lay there and then looked back again . . . looked back at the door, which had opened so suddenly beneath her weight.

It was standing wide open to the tunnel beyond.

Dazed, Jenny lifted herself onto her elbows and realized she was sprawled on a straw-covered floor.

A single candle burned in one corner, just enough light to show crumbling walls . . . a shadow-filled ceiling . . . one tiny window with bars . . .

"Oh, my God . . ."

Jenny got slowly to her feet. Now she could see the rusty manacles upon the walls . . . the heavy chains lying along the floor . . . the pointed hooks suspended from the beams of the ceiling. As something rustled beside her, she whirled around with a cry. Three huge rats were gnawing something on the floor . . . chunks of something raw . . . their whiskers matted with blood, their beady eyes glimmering up at her, bold and unafraid. Jenny covered her mouth with her hand and started backing away from them.

And now she knew where the smell was coming from—the putrid stench of death and rot—and as she flattened herself against the wall, she realized she was standing *under* something—something

suspended high in the air, swinging from the rafters
—and her eyes strained through the gloom, and a
terrified scream rose into her throat—

It looked like a cage.

A metal cage in the shape of a human.

With a place for a head . . . a torso . . . legs . . .

Rust had eaten away at the edges, leaving them a
dull reddish brown, and yet there was something
else, too—crusted over the bars—something else
there, stuck and smeared and clotted . . .

In numb horror Jenny watched as a rat slithered
down onto the cage . . .

As he lifted his nose and sniffed . . .

As he burrowed inside—deep, deep into the
shapeless, moldering cloth which could only have
once been someone's clothes.

12

It's called a gibbet," the voice said.

Jenny whirled around, screams echoing through her brain, but her mouth was locked in a mute circle of terror.

She saw a shadow flickering up the wall . . . a human shadow . . . and as she stared, unable to run or even move, it became a real person . . . a familiar person . . .

One of the twins.

"What are you doing here?" he asked quietly.

Jenny's mind spun in a thousand different directions, but before she could come up with something halfway plausible, he smiled.

"Got lost? It's easy to do in this place."

His smile was easy and kind. She realized she was still gripped against the wall, that her mouth was still open. She closed it and tried to think of something coherent to say.

"You shouldn't be wandering around," he scolded, not unkindly. "Hasn't anyone told you how dangerous it is?"

Jenny nodded, but her eyes lifted once more to the awful contraption swinging above her head. His eyes followed hers, and he nodded slowly.

"It seems so real, doesn't it?"

"Real?" At last she found her voice. "Yes . . . real. I thought—"

"It's for the tour, you know. Tourists love dungeons. They love all the strange and horrible things people can think of to do to each other. Do you know how it works?"

Jenny shook her head. "Malcolm?" she whispered.

He nodded, laughing softly. "Of course."

She watched as he walked a few steps closer, as he pointed upward with a thoughtful frown.

"When a person was hung in chains, he wasn't necessarily dead, you see. Often he was very much alive . . . or half alive, depending on the torture he might have suffered before. Then he just hung there . . . forever . . . with no food or water. Hung there until he simply . . . rotted away."

Jenny felt a painful tingling sensation. Looking down, she saw her hands unclench, her fingers straighten, and she wondered if her blood had actually frozen for several panicky moments.

"It's funny that you wandered in here, though." Malcolm gave her a quizzical smile. "It's so late . . . and so out of the way . . ."

"I was exploring," Jenny said quickly. "I lost track of time, and I've never had any real sense of direction." She stared at him a moment, his black pants and boots, a black shirt today instead of white. He brushed a strand of hair behind his ear, and she suddenly remembered the earring she'd seen on the gypsy that morning. *So it* was *Derreck in the gypsy camp . . . Derreck who swore he never threw the knife . . .*

"Perhaps you'd like to see more," Malcolm said, and Jenny glanced around the chamber uneasily.

"Actually . . . I think I've seen enough. I think I'd like to get back now." From the corner of her eye she caught a quick stealthy movement along the wall, and she inched closer to him.

"You . . . don't like rats?" He glanced first to the wall and then back to her strained face.

"No. I'm terrified of them. I tried to tell you last night—that's what started everything in my room."

He was quiet a moment. He seemed to be thinking.

"They are a problem," he said at last. "But not so bad, really, when you take time to know them. To understand them."

"Who would want to?" Jenny shuddered, and she wrapped her arms about her chest.

"Cold?"

She shook her head, swallowing down a sudden wave of nausea. "That . . . that smell. When I came in here, I'm sure those rats were—were—eating something over there in the straw." She shivered again. "You're not going to tell me that's part of the display, too, are you?"

For a moment he didn't answer. He walked

slowly to the center of the floor and held out his arms. "With the rats and the dampness . . . there's always something molding or rotting in these old rooms. Always something dead. Something . . . dying."

Jenny stared at him. She lowered her head and ran her hands slowly down her arms.

"What is it?" Malcolm asked softly. "What's wrong?"

And to Jenny's surprise, she suddenly felt like crying, and it was all she could do to hold back the tears. She just stood there feeling helpless and frustrated, knowing he was watching her, wishing she could leave. . . .

"What?" Malcolm whispered.

She hadn't realized he'd come over to her . . . hadn't realized how close he was. She felt his hands on her shoulders, and she looked up reluctantly into his face—and he was so handsome, his eyes holding hers, the depth of emotion, the strength she saw there nearly taking her breath away.

"You're so perfect." His face lowered, his lips moving lightly against her cheek . . . her ear . . . the pulse at her throat. "So perfect for this place. . . ."

Jenny shut her eyes as ice-hot shivers coursed through her veins.

"What do you mean?" she murmured. "What do you mean I'm perfect for—"

His kiss silenced her, long and warm and deep, his arms holding her tightly, pressing her hard against him, so that she couldn't get away . . . even if she'd wanted to.

Jenny had never felt like this before. As Malcolm's kiss went on and on, all the strength seemed to flow out of her . . . all her will . . . her body magically suspended, floating somewhere in a dream. She never heard the footsteps behind them . . . was never even aware that anything was wrong . . . until she felt Malcolm suddenly stiffen and pull away, one arm still secure around her waist.

"Derreck," he said softly. "How nice to see you."

Jenny whirled in alarm.

She could see the figure standing silently beside the wall, an identical Malcolm looking back at them. For one crazy moment she felt as if she were looking into a mirror, minus her own reflection.

Derreck ran his eyes slowly over her, and Jenny blushed furiously.

"We've been looking for Jenny," Derreck said at last.

Malcolm smiled. "She got lost."

Jenny didn't know what to say. Totally mortified, she gazed back at Derreck, then jumped as Malcolm touched her lightly on the neck.

"What's this?" he asked, keeping his eyes on Derreck.

His twin didn't answer. For a long moment he stood there as if frozen, as if studying them, as if trying to think of something to say. Puzzled, Jenny glanced back at Malcolm and shook her head.

"Derreck said . . . it must have been an accident," she mumbled.

"Did he, now?" Malcolm raised an eyebrow. "That's a scary thought . . . careless accidents at the fair."

"Come on, Jenny," Derreck said. "I'll take you back."

When Malcolm made no move to join them, Jenny hesitated.

"Aren't you coming?"

Again he and Derreck made eye contact. Again he shrugged his shoulders and gave a smile, though Derreck didn't return it.

"It occurs to me that my brother might be jealous," Malcolm said simply.

Jenny looked at Derreck in surprise. She thought his cheeks flushed slightly, but his stare never left Malcolm's face.

"And unfortunately," Malcolm went on, "I've other things to do at the moment. But . . . I'm sure I'll see you again. Soon."

They didn't leave through the tunnel. As Derreck motioned her out, Jenny was surprised to see a door she hadn't even noticed before, an opening hidden cleverly in the wall. *Of course . . . that's how he came in without me knowing. . . .*

She thought about the figure in her room last night—*a hidden door!*—and suddenly she needed to go over it all again, to remember exactly what had happened, but she knew she couldn't handle the panic right now, the terrible fear and confusion. Derreck was moving far ahead of her now, and in her haste to catch up she stumbled and nearly fell.

"Wait," she pleaded. "You're going too fast."

Derreck . . . jealous?

She made herself concentrate on Derreck now, on his flashlight aimed ineffectually at the tunnel floor, the way he blended so perfectly with the shadows, slipping in and out of them so easily, so expertly, almost as if he didn't care that she was following . . . *almost as if he's trying to lose me.* . . .

He stopped so abruptly, she didn't see him.

He grabbed her arms and shoved her back against the wall, and as she opened her mouth to protest, his hand clamped down over it with frightening strength.

"If it were up to me, I'd have you out of here in a second!" he hissed. "You don't belong here—you have no business going *anywhere* in the castle, understand? And if it takes fear to get you to leave . . . then I promise you . . . your nightmare's just beginning!"

13

Ah, Jenny. There you are."

Sir John barely looked up as Derreck led Jenny into the great hall. He didn't seem to notice that she didn't respond to his greeting. Instead he waved her toward a bench, then gestured at Wit to pass her some food.

Jenny sat down next to Wit, her mind whirling.

"Let's scare Jenny to death. . . . The thrill of the game is in the playing. . . ."

Derreck—is he the one who's been trying to scare me?

She saw Wit's quizzical glance as he handed her a bowl. She ladled out some stew, knowing she couldn't swallow a bite. *Derreck just threatened me—isn't that proof enough?* She was still confused, still shaky from Derreck's unexpected outburst, from her discovery of the dungeon, from Malcolm's kiss—from last night's terrors—from her near tragedy today at the fair. *Derreck . . . jealous . . .* Now as she watched Derreck's stony face at the other end of the table, a whole new storm of questions began raging, began pounding at her, and she quickly looked down at her plate. *"Your nightmare's just beginning . . ."*

Unconsciously she put one hand to her neck . . . ran her fingertips along the telltale mark of dried blood. *Something's going on here . . . something very strange is going on in this house . . . and they're trying to frighten me away so I won't find out. . . .* And suddenly such a surge of fear went through her that she gripped her knife and stabbed it into her bread. Beside her Wit gave a smothered yelp of surprise.

"Did you have a good day at the fair, my dear?" Sir John asked politely, still intent on his dinner.

Jenny only halfway heard. Wit nudged her cautiously with his elbow.

"I . . . yes. Thank you," she murmured.

"And did you find it entertaining?"

"Very entertaining."

She jumped as an arm reached around her from behind and filled her glass. Looking up, Jenny saw Nan looking back at her with vacant eyes.

"Thank you," Jenny murmured, then almost as an afterthought, "Thank you, Nan."

The girl stopped. Her eyes narrowed slowly, and she stared hard at Jenny's face.

"Who are you?" she asked. "Where's Malcolm?"

Derreck sat up straight in his chair.

"He's not eating, Nan. He's . . . busy."

Nan pondered this awhile. Finally she nodded, her eyes back on Jenny. "Who are you?" she asked again.

"Don't you remember?" Jenny leaned toward her. "Today . . . in the wagon—"

"She doesn't remember most things," Wit broke in quickly.

"And last night," Jenny tried again. She took a deep breath and plunged on. "Outside when you tried to warn me—"

"Warn you?" This time Sir John looked up. "What . . . warning are you talking about?"

Jenny stared at him. From the corner of her eye she could see Wit's startled expression, could see Derreck's glass stopped halfway to his mouth.

"I . . ." She trailed off uncertainly. Nan's face registered nothing at all.

"Well?" Sir John prompted.

"Well, what I mean is," Jenny stammered, "what I mean is that she warned me about the stairs. She said for me to be careful not to trip and fall."

Jenny could swear that Wit's shoulders sagged in relief.

"You shouldn't have been outside, Nan," Sir John said sternly. "You know you're never to be out after dark." He cast Jenny a sidelong glance. "Our Nan isn't fit to let out, you understand. In her condition, we couldn't take the chance of her wandering off."

"Oh. Well." Jenny nodded lamely. "But she's a very good dancer, isn't she? I watched you today, Nan. Everyone was enjoying it so much."

Something flickered in Nan's expression. She

lifted her arms above her head and began to sway slowly from side to side.

"Now you've done it," Wit mumbled. "We'll have a whole recital on our hands."

"Not now, Nan." Sir John's voice was stern, and the girl froze at once. "You have duties to attend to. Leave us."

Nan did as she was told. Sir John shifted his glare to the other end of the table.

"Now. Would someone care to tell me what Nan was doing out today?"

The silence was heavy . . . threatening.

It went on and on until Derreck finally cleared his throat and looked up at his father.

"She slipped away. And danced. That's all. We didn't think—"

There was a huge crash as Sir John's fist hit the table. Wit just managed to catch his glass as it tipped over.

"You didn't think," Sir John muttered. "That's always it, isn't it—*none* of you *thinks!*"

Jenny held her breath. Derreck looked down at his plate, and Wit plucked nervously at one sleeve. Sir John resumed eating, and the meal continued in strained silence. Jenny was relieved when dinner was finally over. As Sir John left the room and closed the door behind him, she heard Wit let out a long relieved breath.

"Look." He nudged her. "Nothing up my sleeve."

Jenny looked. Wit's cuff was dangling several inches past the end of his fingertips so that he appeared to be missing his arm.

To Jenny's surprise, Derreck slammed his napkin onto the table and swore under his breath.

"I hate him," Derreck muttered.

"Derreck," Wit said softly, "come on—"

"We're as bad as he is!" Derreck leaned toward them, his voice sinking dangerously. "You know it as well as I do! And her"—he pointed angrily at Jenny—"she—" Abruptly he shook his head and shoved his chair from the table. "I can't go on with this anymore. I really can't."

"Derreck—" Wit tried to grab his arm, but Derreck stormed out of the room.

For a moment Jenny sat there, staring down at the table. Finally she raised her eyes to Wit and saw that he was watching her.

He gave a screech and pulled a playing card from his other sleeve.

"Joker's wild," he deadpanned.

"Wit . . . what's going on?"

"Going on?" Wit echoed. "Going on? In which part of the world? It's all so relative, you know— there's always something going on somewhere."

"Be serious. Please."

He opened his mouth, hesitated, then shut it again. He leaned slowly back in his chair and ran one hand through his hair.

"I can't be serious," he said. "Seriousness makes you old. Unhappy. So why would you want us to be serious?"

"Tell me about Nan," she urged him.

Wit's glance was uneasy. "What about Nan?"

"You said there weren't any women at Worthington Hall."

"I said they either die or go insane or disappear."

Wit's smile was grim. "I think you can guess where Nan fits in."

"Is she really . . . crazy?"

Again he looked at the door. This time his voice sank. "I don't want to talk about Nan."

"Why not?"

"She . . . I just don't."

"Then at least just tell me who she is. Is she related to you?"

"No. She's . . . she just works here."

Jenny pondered this a moment, then voiced her question out loud.

"She doesn't seem the type that your father would have working for him. He's so . . . particular."

"She's simple and slow. She does whatever she's told, and she doesn't ask questions." His face hardened. "Even you should have noticed by now, the king of the castle demands strict loyalty and obedience."

He broke off abruptly and held out his hand as if to ward off further questions.

"I told you. I don't want to talk about Nan."

"Then tell me about the others."

"What others?"

"The other women at Worthington Hall. The ones who never survived."

"A strange bedtime story to request." Wit raised his eyebrow. "Especially right before spending another night alone in the tower."

"You made the whole thing up, didn't you?" Jenny looked levelly into his eyes. "The three of you made the whole story up to scare me."

For a moment Wit looked confused, as if he were

trying to think of something to say. Jenny rushed on.

"You made it up just like you make up other stupid tricks to play on people . . . to scare people. Why, Wit? You said your father doesn't like outsiders, but I'm beginning to think it's not just him who's antisocial around here. Why don't you want anyone coming to Worthington Hall?"

"I didn't make it up," Wit said calmly, but his eyes turned away from her and focused on the shadows near the ceiling. "Not all of it, anyway."

He thought several moments before going on.

"The legend started hundreds of years ago. In England. At the original Worthington Castle. The first mistress supposedly lost her head. I mean"— he pulled one finger slowly across his neck— *"literally*—lost her head."

Jenny suppressed a shudder. "How?"

"It seems her husband—the duke—was an extremely jealous man. But not so loving or romantic to suit her tastes. At any rate, the lady took a lover. And when her husband found out . . ."

Jenny shook her head slowly. "He couldn't have. His own wife?"

"He was what you'd call the jealous sort. If he couldn't have her, then nobody else could have her, either."

"But . . . is that really true?"

"As true as all legends are true." Wit smiled mysteriously. "It set a . . . precedent, shall we say. For all the women who'd come afterward. Something always happened to them—not just to family members, but to servants, as well . . . even female travelers who stopped there for the night. And it wouldn't necessarily happen right away—oh, no. Some would meet strange fates farther down the road. But all strange . . . and horrible."

"But it could have been coincidence, couldn't it? I mean, back then, with ignorance and superstition—"

"Who can tell? All I know is, that's what the *legend* says. Some women were brave enough to challenge the curse and went right on marrying into the Worthington bloodline. Bore Worthington sons and daughters. But they always met a tragic end, sooner or later. And they always saw the ghost before it happened."

"Or so you've heard." Jenny gave a nervous smile.

"Or so I've heard. Some were found in their beds, smothered in their sleep. Or stabbed . . . or poisoned. Some fell from the highest walls of the towers, crushed on the rocks below or drowned in the moat. Some went completely insane, as if they'd witnessed something so horrible, their minds never recovered from the shock of it. And then there were those who disappeared . . . and were never found again."

Jenny stared at his face. A strange solemn expression had crept over his features, and almost mechanically he reached up and removed his cap. Its bells jingled eerily as he placed it upon the table between them.

"And you still believe in it?" Jenny asked, leaning toward him. "This curse?"

"Some do."

"Even though it's just a crazy story?"

"Is lunacy logical?" Wit's laugh sounded forced. "I'm not sure about that one, are you?"

"What . . . what do you mean?"

"I mean a streak of derangement, a freak of nature." His tone was grim, and he cast her a sidelong glance. "It ran in the family and runs there still . . . with eyes that watch and hands that kill—"

Abruptly he broke off. Jenny saw the tense lines around his mouth . . . the stiff set of his shoulders.

"You're trying to tell me something, aren't you?" she said slowly. "You're not just making this up—"

"Oh, dear—oh, dear—what to believe?" Wit jumped to his feet and made a face at her. "Should you stay or should you leave?"

"I want to talk about this," Jenny insisted, but Wit was pulling on her arm, forcing her to stand up.

"No more stories. Instead it's time for bed—"

"Wit—please be serious—"

"I can't, it's impossible, I'm just a fool—"

"Wit!"

Frustrated, Jenny went along with him as he practically dragged her through the halls toward the tower.

"Wit—" she tried again, "about the ghost of Worthington Hall—"

"The one you don't believe in."

"Last night I think I would have believed in anything." Jenny tried to jerk free of him, but he only gripped her harder and hurried her along the passageways. "But now I think someone's deliberately trying to scare me away from here. And I think all the weird things happening might have something to do with Derreck!"

"Derreck!" This time Wit threw back his head and laughed.

"Yes," Jenny said indignantly. "He practically told me so himself. He hates me being here, and he wants me to leave."

"When did he—practically—tell you that?"

Jenny stopped. "Today. This evening."

"And how do you know it was Derreck?"

"I . . ." Jenny's eyes widened. "I just do."

"*How* do you?" Wit persisted. "Did you look at his ear? Did you see the scar?"

"Well . . . no."

"Then how do you know it wasn't Malcolm you talked to? They're always trading places, those two . . . just for the fun of it. Anyone who believes what either of them says . . . is more a fool than I am!"

Malcolm's kiss . . . Malcolm's touch . . . my God, could that have been Derreck?

"Malcolm wasn't wearing an earring!" Jenny burst out.

"An earring? And when was that?" Wit laughed again. "Silly girl, earrings come off just as easily as they go on."

Jenny's mouth opened, and she stared at Wit in dismay. *Anyone who believes what either of them says . . .* Her cheeks flamed furiously, but when she tried to turn away, Wit forced her back.

"I know that look." His eyes narrowed suspiciously. "Oh, no . . . oh, no . . . I do *know* that look!" He rolled his eyes to the ceiling and gave a long-suffering sigh. "All right," he demanded. "Which one?"

"Which one what?" Jenny mumbled.

"Which one"—automatically he began counting off on his fingers—"kissed you, professed his love for you, propositioned you, swore he'd die without you, caused you to swoon in his arms, made your heart race with excitement, arranged for a secret rendezvous, or, put more simply, added you to his endless list of devoted female admirers and—"

Jenny's slap was so quick, so furious, that it surprised even her.

Shocked, she looked into Wit's face and saw the frozen smile there . . . the flicker of hurt in his eyes.

"All right," he said softly, stepping back from her. "All right, then. Perhaps you'll be different. Perhaps you'll be different from all the rest. I hope so. For your sake."

Jenny couldn't stop shaking. As Wit waited for her outside the bathroom, she ran the cold water and splashed it again and again over her face. It didn't make her feel any better. As she and Wit went on to the tower, neither of them spoke a word.

Jenny waited unhappily in the center of the room while Wit lit some candles.

"I'm sorry," she said. "That was horrible of me."

Wit didn't answer. He went back to the doorway and stood staring a moment, out into the shadows.

"It's—" Jenny made a futile gesture with her hands and looked at him pleadingly. "It's just that so much has happened, I don't know what to think about anything. I don't know who to believe. After last night . . . and then the knife today . . . and . . . " She wanted him to turn around and look at her, but he wouldn't, so she rushed on. "And then today I saw him again—the ghost—the executioner. He was *real*, Wit. Only this time he was in the woods behind the fair, and he chased me and I ran! And then . . . well . . . that's when I got lost. So when Malcolm found me in the dungeon and he . . . well, he . . ."

This time Wit turned slowly to face her. His face looked puzzled and strangely pale.

"The dungeon?" he said quietly. "You said Malcolm was in . . . the dungeon?"

"Yes. I—I got lost and ended up in this horrible room, but then Malcolm came in and told me how it was all made up to look real for the tour and—"

She broke off. In the dim light Wit's face seemed to drain even whiter.

"What?" Jenny whispered. "What is it?"

Wit shook his head and started out the door, but Jenny grabbed his arm and tried to pull him back.

"What is it!" she cried. "Something's wrong and you're not telling me!"

He wouldn't answer. With one quick movement he broke free of her grasp and slammed the door shut behind him.

Jenny stood there, stunned. For one minute she thought about taking a candle and going after him, but the thought of maneuvering those treacherous steps again stopped her cold.

She opened the door and stared out into the

darkness. *I think I could do it . . . I think I remember the way this time. . . .*

A sluggish draft crept up the stairwell, and she gasped and shut the door. *But what if the candle goes out? All it takes is one wrong step . . . one wrong turn . . .*

Jenny walked over to the window and looked out. There was a moon tonight, but a veil of clouds hung over it, turning it sallow and gray.

Someone's at the door. . . .

As a cold chill snaked through Jenny's veins, she turned around slowly, her eyes wide.

She heard the bolt being drawn outside, and her heart leapt into her throat. *They said they'd lock me in . . . I didn't think they meant it. . . .*

"Wit!" she called frantically. She ran over to the door and pounded it with her fists. "Wit, you can't do this to me! Open the door!"

She pressed her ear against the thick wood.

No sound from the other side.

"Wit, *please!* I'm so sorry—don't *do* this!"

The latch moved.

It rattled as if someone had touched it . . . as if someone were hesitating on the other side. . . .

For one hopeful moment Jenny actually thought he was letting her out.

But then she heard footsteps—slow and deliberate—growing fainter and fainter down the stairs.

14

Jenny wasn't sure how long she stood there, her forehead pressed against the door, her palms flat upon the wood, feeling sick and empty inside.

Oh, Wit . . . please . . . please come back. . . .

What had she done to upset him so much? Somehow she knew it wasn't just the slap—somehow she knew it had something to do with the dungeon, with Malcolm—because she could still see that strange look on Wit's face when she'd told him about it. *Something about Malcolm . . . oh, Wit . . . what's going on?*

Jenny turned and put her back against the door.

She let her eyes travel slowly around the encircling walls . . . over the window . . . across the foot of her bed . . .

I'm not going to be afraid. . . . I refuse to be afraid. . . .

She closed her eyes and drew a deep breath.

But what if I hear the rats again? . . . What if the ghost comes back? . . .

But he wasn't a ghost, she was sure of that now. He was real.

"So you'll have to guess which of us is which . . . and who is doing what. . . ."

"I don't believe in ghosts," Jenny said fiercely. "I believe someone's trying to scare me, and I'm going to find out why."

It made her angry to think of it again, and she was glad to feel angry, because then she *couldn't* be afraid. Crossing to the fireplace, she stood in front of it and tried to remember exactly where the executioner had stood last night. She could still see the way he'd blended with the shadows . . . the way he'd pulled himself magically out of the darkness. . . .

There's got to be an opening here somewhere.

Jenny slid her hands over the wall, over the roughness of the stones. She leaned into the fireplace and carefully inspected the back of it.

Nothing.

It's got to be here. . . . He had to get in some way. . . .

Straightening up again, Jenny stared at the fireplace and frowned. Just a simple hole in the wall. . . .

Hole . . .

With her heart quickening, Jenny crawled into the fireplace once more, only this time she peered upward, into the flue. *Yes! He must have come down through the chimney!*

Excited now, she reached into the cavity, trying to find a hold so she could boost herself up. Her fingers slid down the sides, and she peered up again in frustration. *There must be something . . . there has to be something. . . .*

She looked around the room and noticed the table beside her bed. After dragging it to the fireplace, she pushed it in, then tested it with her weight, relieved when it seemed sturdy enough. Carefully she climbed on top of it and reached into the chimney. Now she could feel something on both sides—small niches deep enough to hold on to. She ran her hands higher along the flue and found more of the small, uneven ledges . . . and still more . . . like a crude ladder carved into the stone. Jenny hoisted herself up and wedged her feet in the first crevice. It was so dark—frighteningly dark—but she knew she couldn't climb and hold a candle at the same time. Swallowing hard, she pulled herself up to the next two ledges and braced her feet on the walls. *I must be crazy—what if he's on his way down and we run into each other?*

The thought was so terrifying, she almost let go. Catching herself in time, she gritted her teeth and forced herself to go on. *I've got to do this. . . . I've got to see where this leads. . . .*

It seemed to take forever. As Jenny moved slowly, inch by painful inch, her face grew sticky with spiderwebs, and sweat poured down her face. From time to time she felt something crawl over her legs, and it was all she could do to keep from screaming. She remembered the squeals she'd heard the night before . . . the scurrying feet . . . and in her mind she could suddenly picture the chimney swarming with rats, a furry flood of them, raining down on her head.

"Stop it!" she told herself angrily. "Don't think about anything."

But she couldn't help it. She thought of everything that had happened since she'd been here . . . relived every terror . . . and suddenly it hit her how really closed in she was, suspended there in the pitch blackness, with nothing around her but the crumbling walls of the tower—

A black cloud swept through her mind, and Jenny swooned, clutching frantically at the gouges along the flue. She felt as if she was going to be sick, and she froze there, her eyes clamped shut, her breathing loud and harsh, her fingers digging into the stone.

"Go on," she whispered. "You can't stop now. . . ."

With all her strength she reached up again.

Her left hand found another hold.

Her right hand touched nothing but air.

Jenny's eyelids flew open, and her choked cry echoed eerily through the chimney. Angling herself sideways in the cramped space, she was able to lift her head just high enough to see the pale shaft of light glowing down across her arms, to feel the cool breath of air upon her hands.

A window?

For a moment Jenny thought she was dreaming. As she summoned her last ounce of strength, she reached for the open space, found the ledge there, and pulled herself up the rest of the way.

Dangling there from the narrow sill of the opening, Jenny gazed out upon a ghostly scene.

She seemed to be at the very top of the castle. On every side long gray battlements lay deserted in the moonlight, their walls forming crenellated patterns against the sky. Like huge old gravestones, more turrets rose up around her with doorways as empty and black as crypts, and as the wind sighed mournfully along the walkways, shadows and long-dead spirits merged and became one with the darkness.

Jenny pulled herself onto solid ground.

She lay there until her heart stopped racing, and then she got up and walked slowly over to the wall.

The view took her breath away.

It was a sheer drop to the moat far, far below.

So this is how he came in . . . but where did he come from?

Something rustled behind her.

Gasping, Jenny whirled around, her eyes frantically searching the windswept battlements. She could swear she'd heard the sound of a footstep just then . . . the scrape of a heel against stone . . . as though some phantom archer had passed very near to her, keeping restless watch upon the surrounding hills.

After a long moment Jenny started breathing again. She glanced back at the wall and saw that some of the stones had crumbled and fallen away. *My God . . . if I'd leaned against them . . .*

Shuddering, she moved away from the wall and began to slip through the shadows.

She wasn't sure what she was looking for.

She didn't even know where she was going.

The wind was strong up here, almost cold. It blew the clouds thicker and thicker across the moon until there was hardly any light at all. Jenny stopped and put out her hands to steady herself. The shifting shades of darkness made her feel unbalanced somehow . . . disoriented. She saw the walkway like a dream ahead of her . . . and then it disappeared.

I better go back—it was stupid of me to come here—what was I thinking—

But before she could turn around again, she saw the light.

It caught Jenny by surprise—the last thing she expected to see up here in this empty, forgotten place. She saw it shimmering in the distance . . . floating . . . just a pinpoint of hazy brightness beckoning her before it suddenly went out.

Jenny followed it.

She walked fearfully along the battlement, and she saw another tower rising above her, and suddenly she was thinking about death and decay, thinking about dying, and she didn't know why, except the tower was so hideous, so frightening, rotting quietly to pieces beneath the sickly moon . . .

Someone laughed.

It was a strange, cruel laugh, and Jenny hugged the tower wall, pressing herself into the stone.

"Let them come," a voice whispered gleefully. "Up and down the stairs . . . round and round the towers . . . They'll never find *you*. . . . They'll never find *any* of you!"

Jenny went cold all over.

Beside her the tower door yawned open, macabre shadows leaping up the inner walls, dimly showing steps in a downward spiral. *That's where he is . . . whoever's holding the candle . . . somewhere down below . . .*

For a long moment there was silence.

Then suddenly she heard a different sound—jagged and scraping—as though something heavy was being forced across a rough surface.

"They won't know," the voice whispered again. "Because I'm so clever! Much too clever for all of them! To be this close—and not—*ever*—to know!"

The tower echoed with wild, weird laughter.

It floated out into the night and wrapped around Jenny like a cold shroud.

Jenny clutched the wall, fighting to shut out the maniacal sound, but it hung in the air long after the whispering stopped and the light had disappeared.

15

A raw, damp wind shivered along the walkway.

The moon crept from behind its clouds and fell weakly across the entrance to the tower.

I've got to go in there. . . . I've got to find out what's going on. . . .

Jenny couldn't help herself. Even though every nerve and muscle was taut with fear, she knew she had to look inside, to try and make sense of what she'd just overheard. For a long while she stood gazing up at the moon, as if drawing strength from what feeble light it could give her. Then she leaned cautiously through the doorway.

The stairwell lay silent as a tomb.

Looking back once more over her shoulder, Jenny went inside.

She couldn't believe her luck. Almost immediately she spotted a candle and some matches lying near the threshold. *Someone either dropped them*

. . . or keeps them here for a reason. Thankfully she held the wick to a match, breathing a sigh of relief as it burst into flame. Another few steps and she was totally out of range of the moonlight.

She could see now that the tower was little more than an enclosed landing, with the usual stone stairs winding down into endless darkness. She had no idea where the whispers had come from—how far down the speaker had been standing—and so she went slowly, holding the candle high, letting her eyes wander carefully over every inch of the wall and down to each crumbling step.

I know I heard something—something scraping—

With a sinking feeling, Jenny realized how impossible this was—the tower was in such a state of disrepair that even if anything *were* unusual or out of place, she wouldn't have the slightest clue. *I don't even know what I'm looking for—*

She stumbled on one of the steps, and as it teetered sideways, she hopped down to the next and grabbed for the wall. *This is crazy—every one of these old steps is probably loose—I'm going to end up killing myself—*

And then she knew.

Whirling around, Jenny looked back at the step she'd nearly fallen from. She shoved her candle out in front of her, and she held it there a long, long time. At first glance it looked like all the other steps, only now from this angle she could see it seemed a bit askew, dislodged by her foot.

My foot . . . or something else?

She shut her eyes and took a deep breath. It *had*

been a scraping sound, hadn't it? As of something being shoved across an uneven surface— something heavy and awkward to lift—*stone against stone?*

Jenny's pulse began to race. Lowering her candle, she climbed two stairs back. She squatted down and set the candle on the edge of the step, leaning forward with a frown. Just where the step rested there was a crack running below its front edge, along its entire width . . .

Yet it was more than a crack . . .

The jagged line was wide and split, as though part of the stone had worn away and something hollow lay behind.

Jenny put her hands against it and shoved.

It didn't move.

Clenching her teeth, she shoved again, harder.

This time there was a dull grating sound as the step ground itself against the foundation beneath.

That's it—that's what I heard!

Excited now, Jenny put all her strength into it, every muscle quivering from the strain. She could feel a section of the step giving as she leaned into it. . . . She could feel it sliding sideways. . . .

She could see the black hole beneath it.

Exhausted, Jenny drew back, fumbling for her candle. The flame sputtered dangerously, and she whirled in alarm. A breeze? Just a draft along the tower stairs . . . *or something else?*

She held her breath and waited.

Nothing.

No sound . . .

No movement . . .

Nothing.

After what seemed an eternity, she began to breathe normally again, and she turned back to her work.

She held her candle to the gaping hole and squinted her eyes, trying to see what was inside.

Shadows lay black as pitch. Deathly still.

Jenny stared at them. She could feel sweat pouring off her forehead. . . . Her heart was racing so fast, she felt sick.

But I have to see . . . I have to . . .

She scrunched herself tightly against the opening. With every ounce of courage she thrust her candle inside as far as her arm could reach.

For one long moment the darkness held.

It closed over her hand and swallowed up the candle.

And then . . . slowly . . . it began to flicker . . . to melt . . . to ooze back into hidden corners . . . uncovering what it had guarded for so long. . . .

Jenny looked right into their faces.

She saw their empty sockets staring back . . .

And as she screamed and screamed, the rotting skulls grinned up at her with secrets they could never tell.

16

"Are you there?"

Jenny shook her head slowly and curled herself into a small, tight ball.

"Are you there? Answer me—where are you?"

I really am losing my mind—I'm hearing voices —the skulls—the skulls are talking to me—they're trying to get out—they're—

"Where are you?"

The voice was real.

Real and very close.

It floated up the stairwell . . . echoed off the walls . . .

"Oh, my God—" Jenny whispered.

She jerked upright, her hand to her mouth. She didn't know how long she'd been crouched there on the steps, her arms clenched around her stomach, her mind totally dark. *Skulls! Someone hid those skulls under the step—*

"Are you there?" the voice called again, and Jenny could hear the footsteps now, light and hesitant, coming up from the bottom of the tower.

She was afraid to move. Afraid if she made the slightest noise she'd give herself away. *And then what? Am I going to be next? Hidden under the steps with the others?*

With a will of their own, her eyes moved slowly back to the space beneath the stair . . . focused in again upon the yawning black hole. *Why did I say that? I must be losing my mind—I don't know anything about these skulls—maybe they're part of the tour—like the dungeon and the rats are part of the tour—like what's left in that gibbet is part of the tour—*

"Come out," the voice called. "Come out to me."

"Nan?" Jenny whispered, recognizing the sound.

Was the girl alone? Jenny knew she couldn't take the chance.

She grabbed her candle and started to run, but something pulled her back. Panicking, she saw her T-shirt snagged on the wall, and she tried to yank it free. Sallow light flickered up the stairwell . . . a human shadow pulsed across the stones. Jenny tore at her shirt—heard the rip of cloth—but before she could escape, Nan's face appeared on the step below, eyes round and dark and empty.

Like the skulls, Jenny thought suddenly—*just like those skulls beneath the stairs . . .*

"Is it you?" Nan's voice was barely a whisper. The eyes were so large and vacant that they sent chills up Jenny's spine.

"It's Jenny." Jenny tried to keep her voice calm. "Do you remember me, Nan? Jenny. I . . . I watched you dance."

The eyes never wavered. They stayed on Jenny's face, and in their blackest depths there was a strange glint of candlelight.

"Are you looking for him?" Nan asked quietly.

Jenny was afraid to move. She kept her eyes on Nan's face and asked just as gently, "Him?"

"He comes here, you know. He goes wherever he likes."

Jenny nodded. "I think . . . maybe . . . he was just here."

Nan's face clouded. She blinked once, but her eyes remained on Jenny.

"You mustn't tell them. You won't, will you?"

"Tell . . . who?"

"Promise. You won't. Will you."

"No," Jenny said.

"Swear."

"I swear."

Nan gave an almost imperceptible nod. Her eyelids lowered, but her stare seemed fixed on Jenny.

"He likes you. I know because he told me."

Again a slow chill worked its way up Jenny's spine.

"Who does, Nan?"

The girl's eyes widened once more. She looked surprised.

"Why, *you* know. You talk to him."

"I talk to lots of people here," Jenny said carefully. "Which one do you mean?"

"Him."

Nan opened her mouth . . . hesitated . . . glanced over her shoulder into the stairwell beneath.

"You can't tell by his face," she whispered. "You never can tell what he's thinking."

Jenny reached out slowly and touched the wall for support.

"You mean . . . Malcolm? Or Derreck?" she asked softly.

Nan smiled. She shook her head.

"He won't like it if I say. He'll hurt me."

"I won't tell him," Jenny urged. "I promise I won't say anything to him—I won't even tell him I saw you tonight."

Nan looked down at her feet. She raised her eyes to Jenny, but her head didn't move. In spite of herself Jenny took a step back from her.

"Nan," she said softly, "please don't look at me that way—"

"He likes you. He hides where you don't know. He watches when you think you're alone. But he's only waiting. It's only a matter of time, you see. . . ."

"Only a matter of time for what?" In spite of herself, Jenny's voice rose. In the back of her mind she could hear it mocking her from the tower walls. "Nan—please tell me what you mean!"

"They wouldn't come if they knew." She sighed. "None of them would ever come here. Some of them *did* come, and then they never left. Because of him." She shook her head sadly. "It's always . . . because of him."

"Nan—"

"I don't mind." She smiled then, a strange sad smile. "I love him . . . I take care of him. Even when he hurts me. Even when I know that someday he'll—"

"Nan,"—Jenny moved towards her—"Nan, please tell me—"

Slowly Nan backed against the wall, her small body pulling tightly into itself.

"I know he will," she whispered, and her voice was so much more than just sad—it was resigned, Jenny realized with a start—so hopelessly, horribly *resigned*. . . .

"Come back to my room with me," Jenny coaxed. "We can sit down and talk. Wouldn't you like that?"

But Nan was shaking her head, holding out her hands, trying to keep Jenny at arm's length—

"I've always known," Nan murmured, and her words were so quiet that Jenny could hardly hear. "I know he will"—and the huge dark eyes gazed deep, deep into Jenny's face—"because he told me he would."

"Oh, Nan—"

"He knows where you are," Nan whispered. "He knows everything. . . . He's not what he seems." For the first time her voice sounded frightened. "Have a care."

And then before Jenny could answer, Nan turned and vanished, as swiftly and silently as a ghost.

17

Jenny saw dangers lurking in every shadow.

As she hurried back along the battlements to her tower, she could swear that hidden eyes followed her in the dark . . . that muffled footfalls echoed her every step. *Nan . . . oh, Nan . . . what were you trying to tell me—what did you mean? I'm scared for you—I'm scared for both of us—*

Somehow she found the opening again . . . somehow she managed to climb back down the chimney. She was shaking all over, and it was hard to hold on to the wall. Several times her fingers slid from the crevices and she nearly fell, but was able to brace herself with her feet. *Is someone in my room—him?—waiting for me there—waiting for me to crawl out—wondering where I've been?* Near the bottom of the flue Jenny hesitated, every muscle aching, her heart thudding in her chest. She strained her ears through the silence but heard nothing. *"He hides when you don't know . . . watches when you think you're alone. . . ."*

Who, Nan? Who does?

As Jenny lowered herself into the fireplace, she could see her room just as she'd left it, the candle by her bed burned down nearly to nothing. *Maybe he came while I was gone. . . . Maybe he was up there all the time listening to Nan and me. . . .*

A fierce chill shook her from head to toe, and Jenny climbed into bed, pulling the covers up to her chin. She didn't bother changing clothes. She kept her eyes glued to the fireplace, her ears trained to the silence. *He might come back tonight. . . . He might still. . . .*

What could she do? If he really *had* come down the chimney that last time, how could she stop him now? She got up again and repositioned the table beneath the flue. She gathered up all the remaining candles and lit them, one by one, and put them all on the table in the fireplace. Standing back to view her work, she realized how ineffective it all seemed . . . yet it was the best she could come up with.

She sat in bed with her back against the wall, and she kept watch.

She heard Nan's voice replaying a thousand times in her head . . . *"You can't tell by his face. . . . You never can tell him apart. . . ."*

What did it all mean? She could still see Derreck's face that morning as he'd aimed the knife at her head . . . could still feel the slice of the blade against her skin. She could still feel the intensity of Malcolm's kiss as he'd held her in the dungeon, as he'd made her feel as no one had ever made her feel before. . . . *Nan . . . Nan . . . if only you could tell me . . .*

She could still remember the fear in Nan's eyes . . . the terrible, calm surrender in Nan's voice . . . *"Even when he hurts me . . ."* She pressed her hands to her head and tried to shut out the awful images, but they pounded away at her brain, ruthless and frantic. *"Even when I know that someday he'll . . ."*

What, Nan, what?

What did he tell you he was going to do to you?

For one wild second Jenny thought about escaping and taking Nan with her. She could leave in the morning—go to the fair—convince Nan to come along—hitch a ride with someone into town—

And then what?

Frustrated, Jenny knew there was nothing she could do. Getting Nan to come along quietly would be the hardest part, if Jenny could even find the girl in the morning. And then if they went to the police, what could they say that would be believable? *I think someone's trying to scare me. . . . I think someone's hurting Nan. . . . I think there are bodies buried beneath some stairs. . . . I think someone is dangerous. . . . I think something's going on in that house—*

"My God," Jenny mumbled aloud, *"I sound crazy, even to myself."*

Pictures.

The thought came to her so suddenly that she gripped her pillow to her chest and sat up on her knees.

Of course—*pictures!*

She could take her camera back to that tower and get some photographs of the skulls . . . then she'd have some proof to take with her when she left here. . . .

Tomorrow I'll go . . .

She stopped, frowning. *No . . . not tomorrow. Not in broad daylight with a chance of being seen and caught.*

Tomorrow night. After she was back in her tower room and the night was good and dark. . . .

Jenny wasn't sure if she slept or not. She nodded off once or twice, but most of the time she stared at the fireplace, watching for a black-hooded figure to materialize out of thin air. And when pale light began to creep slowly across the foot of her bed, she realized it was morning at last and nothing had happened to her all night.

Maybe I was dreaming . . . the chimney . . . the skulls . . . Nan . . . Maybe I dreamed the whole thing. . . .

Jenny got up and tried the door.

To her amazement, it opened easily in her grasp.

Someone must have come and slid back the bolt. But when? The thought chilled her to the bone. *Did he come in? . . . Did he come into the room and I didn't even know?*

She heard footsteps ascending the stairs, and she scurried back near the bed. The door opened the rest of the way, and one of the twins stuck his head in.

"Good morning." He smiled. "Breakfast is ready if you're hungry."

Jenny stared at him so long that he dropped his eyes and looked himself over.

"What?" He sounded amused. "Did I leave something undone?"

"Malcolm?" she asked weakly, and he gave a chuckle.

"Very good." He nodded approvingly. "You're getting very good at this, aren't you?"

"Malcolm . . ." She stared at him. She wanted to ask him about the dungeon . . . about what had happened yesterday . . . but suddenly she was afraid.

"Yes?" He was watching her curiously. He looked so incredibly handsome this morning, his dark hair, his dark eyes, his romantic clothes. Jenny swallowed hard and tried again.

"When . . . when I saw you in the dungeon yesterday . . ."

He said nothing for several seconds. He seemed to be choosing his words carefully. He gazed down at the floor, then up again into her face.

"About what happened—" he began, but Jenny stopped him.

"No. Please don't apologize. It's just that . . ."

She stared at him helplessly. What could she possibly say that wouldn't sound suspicious?

"Well . . ." Again he hesitated. Again he looked at the floor. "It might have been a good thing . . . Derreck coming in when he did, I mean. He said I might have been . . . out of line." Malcolm raised his eyes to hers. "But . . . you didn't seem to mind. . . ."

Jenny blushed. This time it was she who lowered her eyes . . . and as she did so, she saw Malcolm's boots coming toward her. He stopped, so close she could hear the soft sound of his breathing. She felt his strong, lean body against hers . . . the warmth of him through her clothes. She trembled as his fingers slid beneath her chin and tilted her face slowly up to his.

"May I?" he murmured.

She felt herself nod . . . felt his lips close over hers, even more passionate than yesterday, drawing her breath away, her strength, her will. *Why did I ever think anything suspicious about you, Malcolm? How could I ever have?*

She knew the kiss was ending, yet he didn't pull away. Instead he pressed her head gently against his chest and stood there, holding her. In the protective circle of his arms, Jenny felt as if nothing could frighten her, could harm her, ever, ever again.

"You'll be leaving soon, won't you?" His lips moved lightly against her hair, and she couldn't help shivering.

"Yes. Dad should be back tomorrow."

Was it her imagination, or had she detected a note of relief in his voice?

Malcolm said nothing for a while. Then she heard him sigh.

"I'll miss you," he said quietly, and then he was drawing away from her, and his eyes seemed thoughtful and sad.

Jenny forced a laugh. "You make it sound as if we'll never see each other again."

Malcolm said nothing. He put his hands on her

shoulders and held her at arm's length. He ran his eyes slowly over her, as though memorizing the way she looked. "We'd better go down," he said. "Everything will be cold."

Puzzled, Jenny followed him back to the main part of the house, but Malcolm left her almost immediately, saying he had important business to attend to. Fortunately the corridor was a familiar one, and Jenny found the bathroom with no trouble. It was when she was coming out again that something caught her eye at the end of the hall.

The tapestry.

The same one she'd noticed her first night here.

It was moving again . . . rustling along the floor.

And this time she knew she wasn't imagining it.

Jenny glanced around nervously, but there was no one in sight. Moving as quietly as she could, she crossed the length of the hall and hesitated beside the huge wall hanging. She reached out and ran her fingers down the finely woven fabric . . . and then she froze.

Voices?

She could hear them, just a soft murmuring, but they sounded very far away.

Holding her breath, Jenny pulled the tapestry out from the wall . . .

And stared at the gaping doorway behind it.

Startled, Jenny stood there for several moments, halfway beneath the tapestry, trying to decide what to do. A clammy breeze wafted out, bringing with it another soft swell of voices, but again she couldn't make out what they were saying.

Mustering all her courage, she let the tapestry fall

143

back into place behind her and moved ahead through the opening in the wall.

Almost immediately she discovered a flight of steps leading down. Jenny followed them to a landing, then kept to another hallway as it twisted deep into the castle. She didn't have far to go. As she rounded the next curve, she came so suddenly upon a room and its occupants that she threw herself back against the tunnel wall, terrified she'd been seen.

The voices continued, unaware.

Pressed back into shadows, Jenny managed to turn her head sideways, just enough to get a good look at what was going on.

One of the twins was there. And Nan. And as Jenny watched in surprise, a camouflaged door suddenly opened in another wall, and Wit slipped into the room.

Neither looked surprised to see him.

The three of them stood beside a table. Wit reached down and picked up a small bottle while the twin—Jenny couldn't tell which one—spoke to Nan urgently.

"You've *got* to do it, Nan, understand? You're the only one who can. No one would ever suspect you of doing anything."

Nan stared first at the bottle, then up at him, nodding in her slow, uncertain way. Her eyes were wide and listless.

"It's not really wrong what we're doing," Wit said gently. "You know that, don't you? It's not like—well, what I mean is, it *is* like—"

He looked helplessly at the twin, who broke in quickly.

"A game, really. Just a game. And once this is done, we're taking you out of here—to a different place."

"You can't stay here anymore." Wit gazed earnestly into Nan's blank face. "And what's going to happen—what's been happening—it's got to be our secret."

"Wit's right. You mustn't say anything." The twin turned Nan by her shoulders to face him. *"Our* secret."

Nan's stare was unblinking. Her eyes never left his.

"No one must know, Nan," Wit whispered. "It could be dangerous."

The twin nodded solemnly. "Believe me . . . it'll be better this way."

Without a word Nan threw her arms around the twin's neck and hugged him tightly. He smiled and hugged her back, and as Jenny watched, Nan broke away again and slipped the tiny bottle into the pocket of her dress. Then she vanished quietly through the hidden door.

Jenny stood there a long time.

She saw Wit pace slowly to the end of the room, his face creased with worry. She saw the twin lean forward onto the table and lower his head between his arms. When he spoke at last, his voice sounded empty.

"I can't believe we're doing this. This whole thing—it's—"

"I know," Wit cut in. "I'm scared, too. We all are."

"It's . . . it's got to happen, though, doesn't it?" the twin whispered hoarsely. "And it's not wrong, what we're doing . . . is it? Not like . . ."

"Murder?" Wit's tone was solemn. He came to a sudden halt, his hands clenching at his sides.

"We've got to," he mumbled. "What other choice do we have?"

18

Jenny didn't wait to hear any more.

With her heart pounding furiously, she hurried back the way she'd come, praying she wouldn't be discovered. *"Not like murder . . . just a game . . ."*

With every step she took, a new stab of fear went through her. She could still see the grim expressions on the boys' faces . . . Nan's blank obedience as she'd picked up the bottle from the table. *"What's going to happen . . . what's been happening . . . our secret . . ."*

I was right, Jenny thought dully. *There is something going on in this house . . . and something horrible is still going to happen. . . .*

She was too confused even to think. Gratefully she came out into the corridor again and went quickly on to breakfast. To her amazement, she found everyone else there before her, seated around the table as if they'd been there for hours.

Jenny froze in the doorway and looked around at their faces: Wit—Malcolm—Derreck—Sir John. They were talking casually among themselves, and as they glanced up at her approach and grew quiet, she had the sudden, eerie sensation that what she'd just seen back there in the secret room had only taken place in her mind.

"Good morning," Jenny said softly, taking her place at the table. "I hope I'm not late."

Wit didn't move the bench out for her this time. As Jenny sat beside him, he shifted his eyes away from her, poured himself some coffee, and sat looking down at his cup. Jenny wondered uncomfortably if it had something to do with the scene she'd just spied upon, or if he was still angry with her for last night.

Nan brought a platter of food and held it silently while Jenny dished some eggs out onto her plate. One of the twins lifted a cup to his lips and winked at Jenny over the rim.

"Good morning, Nan." Flustered, Jenny gave Nan a nervous smile, but the girl didn't respond. After a quick glance at Wit, Nan disappeared through a side door.

"I trust you slept well, my dear?" Sir John inquired politely, but kept on buttering his bread, not waiting for Jenny to answer. "Going to the fair again today?"

"Yes." Jenny thought quickly. "But actually I'm a lot more interested in the castle. I was wondering if I could ask you a few questions."

Jenny felt his split second of hesitation. Across from her the other twin leaned forward slowly and regarded her with steady dark eyes.

"Certainly." Sir John nodded. "Ask away."

"Well, there must be lots of stories people have handed down through the years." Jenny kept her face carefully composed. "More legends about ghosts or restless spirits?" She took a deep breath and plunged on. "Tragic victims . . . or . . . damsels in distress, maybe? Family secrets? Murders? Or . . . hidden bodies? You know . . . things like that. . . ."

Wit stared at her. In a fraction of time the room seemed to grow smaller and smaller, pressing in on her with unseen dangers. One of the twins cleared his throat. The other shifted his gaze onto his father's face.

"I'm afraid," Sir John said, touching a napkin to each corner of his mouth, "that I've not heard any stories such as those. But perhaps the boys have. My imagination, unfortunately, leaves much to be desired."

He pushed back his chair and left the room.

Jenny sat where she was and felt three pairs of eyes upon her.

"Let's go," one of the twins finally mumbled. Obligingly the other got up and followed him out, leaving Jenny alone with Wit.

She put down her fork and gazed at her untouched food.

What am I doing here? Now's my chance. . . . Go down to the fair . . . hitch a ride with someone . . . get away from this place and forget this whole thing ever happened—

"You look like you could use a friend," Wit said. "Even if it isn't me."

Oh, Wit, what were you doing in that room—

*what were you and your brother talking about—
what did you give Nan in that bottle—what's going
on—*

"On the other hand," Wit went on, talking to
himself more than to her, "I'm best at being
friends."

Jenny glanced at him. "I thought you were best at
being clever."

"I'm best at being a clever sort of friend. Shall we
go?"

"No, you go without me."

"And leave you alone in this doom-and-gloomy
place? Why, Malcolm—or is it Derreck?—would
never forgive me!" He ignored the look she gave
him and rushed on. "I know just the thing to cheer
you up. You should go to the tournament."

"What tournament?"

Wit tilted his head back, picked up a piece of
sausage, and balanced it upright on the end of his
nose.

"The one at the fair. Scores of dashing young
knights—Malcolm will be there. Or is it Derreck?
To win a lucky lady's hand." His eyebrow lifted
suggestively. "Maybe *you're* the lucky lady?"

Jenny's cheeks flushed, and she put her hands
casually to her face. *That was Malcolm, wasn't
it—in my room just this morning? Did he have
enough time to get to that secret room before I did?
Or was that Derreck in there conspiring with Wit?*

"Come on." Wit stood up and led her out into
the corridor. The twins were there talking to each
other, their heads down, voices low. As one looked

up and noticed her, the other touched her arm, stopping her before she could leave.

"Jenny—you will be at the tournament?"

Surprised, she looked from one identical face to the other. "I . . . I wasn't planning on it."

She didn't hear Wit come up behind her, and she jumped as he slipped his arm around her waist.

"Of course she will," Wit replied. "What's a feature on fairs without featuring a tidbit or two about tournaments?" He put a finger to his temple, as if thinking. "And what's a tense, terrifying tournament without a lovely luscious lady?"

The twins exchanged amused looks, and Wit held up his hands in a dramatic gesture for quiet.

"And I proclaim—as jester of this court—that *right* now—without a *moment's* delay—*Jenny* should give *Malcolm* a kiss. A kiss for luck."

Jenny's cheeks flamed. She shook her head and felt Wit pushing her forward.

"Oh, go on. It's customary. You wouldn't send a knight to his doom without a token of your affection, would you?"

One of the twins snorted. "Doom! Thanks for the vote of confidence."

"Yes, Jenny, go on." The other leaned back against the wall and crossed his arms over his chest. "Do give—*Malcolm*—a kiss for luck."

Again Jenny shook her head, more firmly this time.

"Don't you get tired of these stupid games? All three of you remind me of little boys—you should have outgrown this stuff a long time ago."

"Do it," Wit challenged her. "How bad can it be?"

Jenny could feel her blush deepening as the twins laughed. Defiantly she reached up to one of them and slid her fingers behind his left ear.

"You're Malcolm," she said. "Satisfied?"

She gave him a perfunctory kiss and pulled back again, glaring at both of them.

"Am I?" The twin sounded surprised.

"Yes." Jenny's voice was adamant. "There's no scar behind your left ear."

To her dismay, the other twin let out a groan.

"Not the old scar thing again, Wit! Can't you be more original?"

"At least it was on the *ear* this time," his brother mused. "Last time it got *really* embarrassing."

As all three brothers burst into laughter, Jenny stormed down the corridor. She refused to turn around, even when she heard Wit running behind, calling her name.

"Come on, Jenny, wait up! It was just a joke!"

"You're a joke," Jenny muttered.

"Thank God I've lived up to my calling!"

Jenny hurried outside and away from the house. The sun was warm and clean, and she wished desperately that it could make everything disappear—her fears, her uncertainties, the house and its riddles and everyone in it.

"I'll race you!" Wit said breathlessly, catching up to her. Jenny knew he could have caught up anytime he'd wanted to and suspected he'd only given her a chance to cool down.

"I don't want to race with you," she threw back

at him. "I don't want to have anything to do with you."

"Oh, so you gave Derreck a kiss. Big deal."

"Maybe that wasn't Derreck. How would you know?"

"Sometimes I *don't* know. Sometimes I have to stop and think. Or look for distinguishing marks."

"Oh? Under their eyelids, maybe? Or on the bottoms of their feet?"

"Excuse me—are we overreacting just a *little*? I was just having fun—"

"Well, nothing personal, but I don't think being made a fool of is fun. And I don't think your house is fun. I think there's something going on there that's definitely *not* fun!"

Jenny stopped. She bit down on her lip and closed her eyes, shocked at what she'd just said. When she opened them again, Wit was looking at her solemnly.

"What? What do you think is going on at our house?"

"Nothing. I didn't mean anything. Just a figure of speech."

"I don't think so. Jenny!"

She started off again, but Wit raced up to her, grabbing her arm, forcing her to stop and look at him. His hair was windblown around his face, and he looked even more boyish than usual—young and confused and—*what?*

"Jenny—please—after I say this, you've got to promise me you'll forget it. You'll pretend it was *never* said. Promise."

She stared at him. She could see that other

emotion struggling beneath his expression, and with a start she suddenly realized it was fear.

"Jenny. Listen to me. There *is* something going on at the house." He was speaking rapidly now, whispering so low and so fast she could hardly keep up with him. He had her by the shoulders, and he was leaning in close to her ear, as though fearful any moment they'd be overheard.

"I can't explain anything right now. You've just got to trust me."

"Trust you? Oh, please. You've given me such good reasons to."

"Forget all that. This isn't a joke, this is real—"

"Haven't I heard that line somewhere before?" Jenny threw back at him. "And it seems to me your answer to that was—"

"Listen. Your father wanted a nice, pretty story —so don't go after any others. Jenny, do you understand? Get your story—then get the hell out of here. Get as far away as you can, promise me. Jenny—please—*promise!"*

Jenny's annoyance turned slowly to bewilderment . . . then to fear. Wit looked so intense, his eyes pleading, his face strained.

"I don't know what's going to happen." His voice sank even lower. "I just know I don't want anything to happen to *you.* None of us do."

Jenny peered hard into his face. There wasn't the slightest hint of teasing there now.

"Please, Jenny," he murmured, and he was pulling her close . . . resting his lips against her forehead . . . smoothing her hair. "I don't want . . . anything . . . to happen to you. Please . . ."

"What is it?" she asked, and there was a cold, heavy feeling in her heart. "Why can't you tell me?"

Abruptly Wit released her. He held both his arms high in the air, then sprang into a series of cartwheels that took him the rest of the way down the hill. Jenny trailed after him in slow motion. She knew it would be useless to question him now. She watched as he landed nimbly on his feet, as he led her into the make-believe.

19

The fair was even more full than yesterday.

Immediately Jenny and Wit were swallowed up by a confusion of modern tourists and medieval characters of every shape, size, and sort—but Wit maneuvered effortlessly through the crowds. For Jenny it was almost painful, seeing the smiles around her—hearing the laughter. . . . *Nobody's even aware that something's wrong . . . It's so heavy, so dangerous, I can feel it in the air, but I'm the only one who knows. . . .*

A horrible premonition lay like a stone in the pit of her stomach. As Wit pulled her along behind him, all the bright colors and happy sounds ran together and became a blur in Jenny's mind. The image of Nan's face kept haunting her . . . the strange warning Nan had given in the tower—*"You can't tell by his face. . . . You never can tell what he's thinking. . . ."*

It could be anyone, Jenny thought with a shock.

How well did she really know them—any of them?

To her they were just faces . . . names . . . separate personalities they allowed her to see. . . .

Sir John . . . Malcolm . . . Derreck . . . Wit . . .

Who was Nan trying to warn me about . . . the one whose face masks his true thoughts. . . .

Jenny stopped abruptly, cold seeping through her bones.

Malcolm's kiss . . . Derreck's warning . . . Wit's friendship . . .

She closed her eyes, one hand going to her throat.

"You'll have to guess which of us is which . . . and who is doing what. . . ."

"Hey, Jenny." Wit was staring at her. "Are you okay?"

"We're very good at keeping secrets. . . ."

"Jenny—" Wit reached out for her, but Jenny pulled away.

"Leave me alone," she said. "I have research to do."

Wit looked surprised. "Oh, come on, if you're still mad about what happened back—"

"Leave me alone, Wit! I want to be by myself!"

"Oh, this is stupid, Jenny, it really is. You talk about *me* playing games . . ." Wit muttered and positioned himself directly in front of her. His hands snapped shut, and he held out two fists. "All right, then. Pick one."

"No."

"Pick one. Or I'll do something to embarrass you in front of the whole fair."

He looked as if he meant it. Hesitantly Jenny chose his left hand, and Wit opened it with a wry smile.

"Derreck has a scar"—he ran his right forefinger along the width of his left palm—"straight across, just here. A most unfortunate souvenir." Wit shook his head in mock sadness. "His hand got in the way of a knife that went astray—but scars give us integrity, don't you think?"

Jenny rolled her eyes and started to leave, but Wit grabbed her.

"I swear that this is true—I wouldn't lie to you!"

"You really are impossible." Jenny shook him off and immediately plunged out onto the packed thoroughfare. After a while she looked back to see if he was following her, but the jester had disappeared.

She didn't see either of the twins at the gypsy camp. Nan wasn't there dancing, either, and as Jenny came upon the tournament area, she kept scanning the crowds uneasily for signs of a familiar face. The sun was growing hot. Excited onlookers spilled from pavilions and viewing stands set around the field where gallant knights and horses faced off in battle. Costumed ladies waved handkerchiefs, and pages hurried to and fro. Jenny walked slowly back beyond the arena, to the tents and stalls where knights were readying themselves for combat. No Malcolm.

Positioning herself behind a big tree, Jenny waited. She waited for fifteen minutes and was just getting ready to leave when she noticed one of the twins suddenly slipping out of the woods and around the corner of a dressing room. *Malcolm?* His clothes were stained and disheveled, and he was out of breath. As a page ran up to help him, he impatiently waved the boy away.

Jenny started toward him, then stopped. From her hiding place, she had a clear view of Malcolm without being visible herself. She saw him yank his shirt off over his head, fling it to the ground, and kick it into a corner even as he grabbed his side and doubled over. Jenny drew her breath in sharply. Malcolm's ribs were bruised, and ugly red scratches crisscrossed his skin. After a long moment he grabbed another shirt from a pile of clothes and slid into it, whirling around suddenly as someone came up behind him.

It was Nan.

To Jenny's surprise the girl grabbed Malcolm's arm, tugging on him as he tried to shake her off. Her face looked pale and frightened, and she was babbling, though Jenny couldn't hear what was being said. For an instant Malcolm froze. He took one step toward Nan, but before he could get any farther, a shouting group of knights ran up and surrounded him. Laughing boisterously, they grabbed his weapons and hustled him off to the arena.

Jenny saw the strange wild look on his face as he glanced back at Nan.

And the way Nan disappeared into the woods again.

Jenny didn't waste any time.

She hurried over to where the two had been standing and picked up the discarded shirt.

It was spattered with blood.

The front of it and one of the sleeves . . . soaked with wet red stains.

Staring down at it, Jenny felt sick. She let the shirt slide out of her grasp and backed away from it, glancing over toward the arena. *"You never can tell what he's thinking. . . ."*

Malcolm was struggling with another knight, both of them locked in hand-to-hand combat. The air throbbed with dust and sweat and the wild screams of the crowd.

Jenny felt frozen; she couldn't look away. She saw Malcolm force the other knight back—she saw the other knight fall to the ground. The stands went into a frenzy. She watched as Malcolm raised his sword high above his opponent's head. . . .

Jenny turned and ran. She didn't know where she was going—she couldn't seem to get a grip on herself. As she plunged recklessly along the packed walkways, she thought she heard someone calling her name, but when she searched for the voice, she didn't see anyone she knew. Someone shoved her backward, and she found herself sandwiched between two street beggars. Jokingly they pushed her back and forth, until at last one of them swung her outward in another direction, and she broke free and ran.

Jenny sped up the hill to the house. The sinister towers of Worthington Hall loomed high above her, silent and withdrawn, guarding their secrets. Just beyond them the sun was easing stealthily behind a mask of darkening clouds. Already Jenny could hear the first faint rumblings of thunder in the distance, and she wondered how long it would be before another storm broke.

She found her way through the main part of the house without any trouble. She called out several times, but there didn't seem to be anyone at home. *Strange . . . I thought at least Nan would be here somewhere. . . .* She wandered along familiar corridors, past the tapestry, then stopped uncertainly at a latched door. She'd been this way twice before now—she was almost sure this entrance would lead to the stairs of her tower room. She pushed the door open and went through.

I should have remembered to bring a light.

She kept seeing the bloody shirt Malcolm had ripped off . . . kept seeing Malcolm's sword poised above the other knight's head. . . .

It's only a game. It's all part of the show.

I don't even know if it was Malcolm. It could have been Derreck. In fact, I'm not sure which one of them has been doing or saying anything to me since the very first moment I've been here. . . .

She looked up at the curving steps of the tower. She thought of skulls hidden beneath stairs . . . of strange laughter and secrets . . .

She felt a hand slowly curling around her own.

Screaming, Jenny slammed back against the wall. She caught just a glimpse of shadow . . . a glint of eyes—

"Asleep," the voice whispered. "He's sleeping now."

Jenny stared as Nan pulled out of the shadows, as the girl's wide eyes focused uncertainly on Jenny's face.

"Nan"—Jenny's breath came out in a rush—
"God—you scared me half to—"

"He won't wake up." Nan reached over and once
again took Jenny's hand.

"Wh-what are you talking—" Jenny broke off
abruptly and stared.

The front of Nan's dress hung in tatters. Her
skirt and bodice were smeared with something
dark and wet. As Jenny shifted her gaze to Nan's
eyes, she saw them fill slowly with tears.

"Oh, Nan, what's happened?"

Without another word Nan took Jenny's arm and
began to lead her down the stairs in the opposite
direction. Jenny hadn't realized how really deep
the tower was—every bit as deep as it was high—
and as they descended farther and farther into the
bowels of the castle, she huddled close to Nan and
held on tight. Nan never hesitated. When at last
they reached bottom, she hurried confidently
through a maze of tunnels, dragging Jenny along
behind. The air was dank and foul, and as Jenny
tried to keep from gagging, it suddenly hit her that
she'd smelled the noxious odor before.

Without warning Nan turned down another passageway, and Jenny's heartbeat quickened. Now
she could see the candles flickering in the niches of
the walls . . . could see the doorway yawning in
front of them with its grisly cavern beyond. . . .

Nan stopped and squeezed Jenny's hand.

"You wake him," she implored. "You try."

She moved ahead of Jenny into the dungeon.

She took a candle from a ledge and held it above
her head.

Jenny saw the gibbet swinging from the rafters. . . .

She saw the rats scurrying away from the candlelight. . . .

She saw Wit sprawled in the corner . . . chained to the wall . . . and covered with blood.

20

~~~~~~~~

Wake up," Nan said softly. "Wit . . . wake up . . ."

In horror Jenny stood there and watched as Nan knelt beside the still figure, as she softly patted his cheek, as she began to sing.

"My God . . ." Jenny murmured. "No . . ."

She fell on her knees beside Wit and touched his face, felt for a heartbeat. His skin was cold and clammy, and Jenny couldn't hear him breathing. Panic-stricken, she looked wildly at Nan and saw only empty eyes staring back at her.

"We've got to do something!" She grabbed Nan and shook her. "We've got to get a doctor—Nan— *listen* to me! Go get the twins—Sir John—we've got to get a—"

Abruptly she broke off. Nan was rocking back and forth . . . smiling . . . singing some off-key lullaby.

"Wit!"

In desperation Jenny began pulling Wit out of his costume, trying to find the source of his wounds. The stench in here was even worse now, metallic with the smell of blood, and as Jenny worked hurriedly to get his shirt off, she saw the rats creep close, their noses lifted in the air.

"Get out of here!" Jenny lunged at them, and the rats scurried deep into the shadows. She turned back to Wit, then gave Nan another sound shake.

"Nan—get some water! *Please,* Nan, listen to me! We've got to get him out of these chains—get some *help!* Who did this? You must know—who *did* this to him?"

For one split instant a flicker of doubt went across Nan's face. She nodded slowly at Jenny, then leaned over and cradled Wit's head in her arms.

"You know," she whispered. "You know who did it."

"I don't know! *Tell me!*"

"Him. The one who hides. The one who watches in the dark."

Jenny's blood ran cold. "Where . . . where did you hear that? Who told you to say that?"

And it came back to her in a sickening rush—her fall down the stairs—the frail arms supporting her, guiding her into that horrible damp place—

"You," Jenny murmured. "*You* were the one who took me there. *You* were the one who picked me up in the hallway—"

"He did it," Nan said again. Her face clouded over, and she pulled her hair down across her eyes.

"You can't tell him apart. You can't ever tell him apart. . . ."

"Oh, my God . . ." A cold rope of fear coiled itself around Jenny's heart. "The twins. You're talking about the twins, aren't you? Nan! Which one of them did this—tell me *which one!*"

To Jenny's dismay, Nan began to sing again, softly, with Wit's head still clutched in her arms. Jenny tore at Wit's shirt and then drew back with a choked cry. She could see the wound now—huge and jagged, ripped flesh and shattered bone. She tried to staunch the flow of blood and saw the dark pool of it spreading beneath him, around him, already thickening in the straw.

"He's bleeding to death." Jenny was shaking so badly, she could hardly get the words out. "You've got to take me back, Nan—we've got to get a doctor."

She reached for the girl, then froze as a soft sound came from Wit's lips. Terrified, Jenny leaned down over him and put her ear close to his mouth.

"Wit—Wit, can you hear me?"

His eyelids fluttered. He shifted restlessly and moaned.

"Wit," Jenny whispered.

And then he looked at her. Jenny could see the strange glaze over his eyes as he tried to focus in on her face.

"Jen . . . Jenny—"

"Yes, it's me! Who did this to you, Wit—why did this happen—"

"You've got to . . . leave." The words came

breathlessly, through clenched teeth. "Promise me. Leave . . . now. Take . . . Nan . . . with you—"

"Wit—I'm going for help, but I'll be right back—"

Jenny jumped to her feet and grabbed Nan. Roughly she thrust the girl ahead of her toward the door.

"We've got to get help, Nan—*now!* Take me back to the house!"

Everything was a dull haze . . . everything empty. As Jenny pushed Nan through the darkness, all she could see was Wit, his blood, his gaping wound —and all she could hear was Nan, singing, saying the awful words—"You can't tell him apart."

"You can't ever tell him apart—"

My God . . .

One of the twins.

"We're very good at keeping secrets . . . which is which . . . who is doing what . . ."

"Murder . . . what other choice do we have . . ."

"Oh, Wit—what's happening? Don't die, please don't die—"

They reached the house at last, and Jenny ran down the corridor to Sir John's study. *I'll call an ambulance—the police—* She burst into the room and stopped cold as one of the twins turned around from Sir John's desk by the window.

"Jenny"—he looked surprised—"is something wrong?"

Jenny stared at him. She stared at him and felt her face drain white.

"I . . . need to use the phone," she whispered.

A clap of thunder exploded beyond the window-pane. Rain streamed against the glass.

"Strange . . ." The twin gave a frown. "I came in here to use it myself, but the damn thing's gone out or something. Must be the storm."

And Jenny could hear it now, could see it raging beyond the windowpane—churning sky, thunder and lightning—the afternoon as dark as night. Someone entered the room behind her, and she whirled around with a cry.

"Bad luck, that." Sir John looked annoyed. "Modern conveniences always go out when you need them most. Is there something I can do for you, Jenny?"

"Sir John—" Jenny backed away from the twin —*which one*—*which one*—and took hold of the old man's arm. "Could you—could you please come with me?"

"With you? Why, what's wrong, you act as though—"

"It's an emergency—there's been an accident," Jenny blurted out, and she was still backing away from the twin, still holding on to Sir John, guiding him out into the hallway.

"An accident? Good heavens, where? *What?*"

"Please—just come with me—just *you*. Just you come. Nan will take us."

"Nan?" His eyebrow raised, and at last he spotted the girl hanging back in the shadows of the hallway. "What on earth happened to you?" he demanded, seeing the condition of Nan's clothes.

Nan lowered her head and shrugged, saying nothing.

"Please—" Jenny prodded him, and he gave her a tolerant nod.

"Oh, very well, then. Yes. Of course."

And again they were winding through the labyrinth of tunnels, only this time Jenny was running, pleading with them to hurry, Sir John muttering under his breath, and she kept looking back, looking back over her shoulder, and *he* was there—one of the twins—following them—running after them through the dark—

"It's Wit," Jenny said breathlessly, and they were at the dungeon now, and she was pushing them inside, and she was pointing at the corner—"It's Wit—he needs a doctor—he—"

And she broke off and felt her mind slam in on itself—felt the silent screaming in her brain as Nan began to sing and sway, as Sir John stood staring at them from the doorway.

"Is this your idea of a joke, young lady?" he asked quietly.

"No," Jenny whispered. "No . . . no . . ."

She couldn't see any chains now . . .

Or rats . . .

Or pools of congealed blood in the filthy straw . . .

Wit was gone.

21

~~~~~~

Jenny gazed numbly into the shadows. She didn't hear the twin come up behind her . . . didn't know he was even near her until she felt his hand on her shoulder.

"What was it," he asked, "that you thought you saw?"

Jenny whirled on him, shaking off his touch.

"I didn't *think* I saw anything! I *know* I saw Wit. He was hurt—bleeding—right there in that *corner!* Never mind what I saw—if you don't believe me, ask Nan—*she's* the one who came and got me and brought me here!"

"If I didn't believe *you,* why ever would I ask *Nan?*" Sir John said dryly.

He cast the girl a patronizing look. She had wrapped her arms about herself and was quietly dancing along one of the walls. Jenny stared helplessly and felt tears of rage burning in her throat.

"He was here. He may be *dying!* Why won't any of you believe me!"

"Good heavens, Derreck." Sir John rolled his eyes. "Kindly inform our guest she's just become another victim of Wit's perverse practical jokes."

Jenny stared at them in total shock.

"This—this couldn't have been a joke!" she sputtered. "This—if you'd seen him—"

"Yes, yes." Sir John afforded her a half-amused laugh. "We've seen it all before. I'm afraid, my dear, that you can never trust your eyes when these boys are around. They're—all of them—fiends." He raised one eyebrow at his son, then disappeared out the door.

For a long moment Jenny stood there, trembling from head to foot. *A joke!* This whole thing—this elaborate charade—Nan—Wit—all of it—a joke! Swallowing hard, she looked up. Derreck was watching her, and she met his gaze defiantly.

"I want to go back to the house," she said.

"Where was he?"

"What?" Jenny narrowed her eyes.

"I said . . . where was he?" Derreck repeated. His dark eyes darted around the room . . . suspicious . . . as if probing every shadow. "When you saw him. Wit."

"Haven't you had enough fun for one day?" Jenny turned on her heel and started toward the door. "Derreck? Malcolm? Or whoever you are?"

He said nothing. Jenny looked back and saw him kneeling in the corner, staring down at the straw.

"Are you coming?" she demanded.

Slowly he got to his feet and led her to the house, neither of them saying a word.

A joke!

Jenny was actually glad to be in her room again. She lit a candle and took a slow appraisal of the empty shadows. She sat down on the bed and buried her face in her hands, her mind whirling out of control.

But Nan's face—the intensity of it when she'd come to take Jenny to the tower. How could that have been a lie?

She was in on it, too—you've seen her—she'll do anything any of those boys tell her to do.

And what Nan had said—*"You can't ever tell him apart"*—how much more of a confession could it be? She'd practically admitted to Jenny that one of the twins was responsible for Wit's injury—

But they're always trying to fool me—mixing themselves up so I can't tell one from the other—and Wit's always teasing me about liking Malcolm—so what better way to turn off my feelings for Malcolm than to stage something disgusting like this and make me suspicious of him?

Jenny lay down across the bed. She couldn't think anymore—she welcomed the numbness. Tears ran down her cheeks, and she let them come, too exhausted to wipe them away. How could they do something like this to her? It was worse than sick—it was—

"Unforgivable," she choked. "I'll never forgive any of them for this. Not ever."

And it came to her then what Sir John had said on the very first night—*"I have an insatiable passion for games"*—and how everything—*every* single thing since she'd been here—the ghost, the skulls, the dungeon, even the overheard conversations—had probably all been just one giant make-believe prank.

Even Malcolm, she thought bitterly.

Even Malcolm's kiss . . .

A roar of thunder shook the tower around her, and she buried her face in her arms. She heard the door open softly, and she heard Nan's voice from the threshold, but she didn't bother looking up.

"Hot tea," Nan said. "Before I go."

"I don't care if you go," Jenny mumbled into the covers. "In fact, I wish you *would* go."

In spite of her annoyance, she finally lifted her head and saw Nan putting a cup on the bedside table. The girl stood back and regarded her quietly, wiping her hands on her dress.

"Tonight," she mumbled. "Tonight is when I go."

"All right, Nan." Jenny sighed. "Since I can tell you want me to ask. Go where?"

But the girl only shook her head. "I told him," she whispered. "He didn't like it at all."

"Who didn't like it?"

"Him."

"Oh, I get it." Jenny gave a grudging nod. "Him again. The one who hides. The one who watches in the dark."

Nan looked puzzled. She gave a slow nod, then turned toward the door.

"Maybe I shouldn't have told," she mumbled under her breath. "I . . . don't think I was supposed to . . . was I?" Again she shook her head. "I . . . can't remember."

Jenny watched the door close. Sighing deeply, she reached for the cup and raised it to her lips. The tea was strong and hot, soothing as it flowed through her body. She could actually feel her muscles unclenching . . . the pressure subsiding behind her eyes. She fell back again across the bed, her thoughts more calm now, picking up where she'd left off. . . .

How could it have been a joke? All the blood— the open wound—*how could it have been a trick?* She stared up at the tiny window and saw jagged rips of lightning slash the sky. The rain was coming down in torrents now, even worse than her first night here. As Jenny continued staring, the window seemed to distort . . . to stretch itself wider . . . then shrink back again. Jenny frowned and rubbed her eyes. The window was normal again.

Maybe it's me . . . With all the strange things going on around here, I'll believe anything. . . .

She rolled over on her back and laid one arm across her eyes. Strange . . . the room seemed to be spinning . . . the walls going around and around in a dizzying circle. She braced her elbows against the mattress and tried to sit up but fell back uselessly onto the bed. She could see the ceiling above her, twirling in a slow, lopsided circle, and she shut her eyes and gripped the covers with both hands. She felt as if she were falling, yet there was no fear, she was wonderfully relaxed.

The tea . . . something in the tea . . .

It came to her slowly, teasing the corners of her

mind, but she wasn't quite able to grasp the meaning of it all. She gave in to the dizziness and let herself drift and drift into the deepest realms of sleep. . . .

She wasn't sure what woke her.

She tried to lift her head, but the room swayed and spun around her, lazily, like a cradle rocking her back to sleep. She peered through the flickering candlelight, around the walls of her empty room.

The photos. I've got to get those photographs.

The thought came to her out of nowhere . . . some hazy memory of something crucial and upsetting. *Wit?* A flash of images snapped on in her brain—*blood and straw and rats and the smell of death* . . . Jenny fought to remember, but just as quickly the images faded again, leaving her groggy and confused. Why had she thought about Wit just then? Did he have something to do with taking pictures?

She got to her feet, holding on to the table for balance. *I can't do this . . . there's no way I can do this. . . . What's wrong with me?* . . . With every ounce of strength she managed to drag the table into the fireplace . . . climb on top of it. She wasn't even aware of thinking it out . . . making a plan . . . only doing it mechanically as if she'd done it before. *Have I? Have I done this before?*

She tried to pull herself up into the flue. Uselessly she dropped back down again and sprawled across the tabletop.

Jenny moaned and gritted her teeth. She concentrated on clearing her head, but everything was swimming . . . swimming . . . Painstakingly she tried once more—and this time managed to wedge herself up into the flue. Her feet and hands scrambled for holds, as if they'd known some were there, and she began to inch upward, niche by niche. She wasn't sure anymore if she was really moving or if she'd drifted off to sleep again and dreamed of climbing.

A draft of fresh air blew across her face, rousing her for an instant. She opened her eyes and saw only darkness and concluded that she really must be dreaming after all. She hung there, limp and sleepy, and began to nod off when another cool breeze crept across her face. This time it brought a soft spray of rain with it, jolting her into a slow awareness. Surprised, she felt the strain of her weight as she held herself against the wall. She looked down into bottomless dark. *Come on, Jenny, come on . . . only a little more . . .*

With a last burst of strength Jenny heaved herself up and found the opening. She fell out onto the battlement and lay there motionless, sucking in deep gulps of windy night air. Lightning ripped the sky above her head, unleashing floods of rain, but she scarcely even felt it.

After a long while she lifted her head.

She thought she saw light dancing far off in the forbidden tower.

She thought she heard someone singing.

Dizzily Jenny groped her way along the walk. She clutched her camera tightly to her chest, not even aware of her soaked clothes, not even aware of the wind buffeting her dangerously close to the edge of the wall. As she slowly neared the turret, she paused in a pool of shadows and rubbed her eyes, thinking they were playing tricks on her.

She could see the human figure silhouetted against the flickering wall. She could see its tall, rigid stance and the small form crouched there at its feet.

Jenny stared.

The shadows merged . . . separated . . . swirled and danced in her muddled brain. . . .

She took a deep breath and willed her mind to clear.

She saw the arm lift high into the air . . . saw the vague outline of a sword, distorted in the candlelight . . .

Sword . . . Malcolm . . .

She saw the blade fall. . . .

The singing stopped.

22

*I am dreaming—I must be dreaming—Jenny—
oh, God, Jenny—you've got to wake up!*

She was trying to run, but she couldn't, trying
not to make any noise, yet she thought she might
have screamed, she wasn't sure. She could hear
herself as from a long distance off, slipping and
sliding over the battlement, crawling along the
stones, falling and getting up again.

Oh, no—oh, no no no—

The wind was beating at her, and rain was pelting
her face, and she tried to look back over her
shoulder, but everything was gone—the light—the
shadows—the singing—*the singing—*

Jenny pulled herself into the chimney and
grabbed for a handhold. Her fingers were slippery,
and she slid down sideways before managing to
catch herself. The walls were wet now, too, just like

her hands were wet, her clothes, her body was wet, chilled and shaking—*wake up wake up wake up*—

She knew somehow that her mind was spinning out of control—*if only I could scream*—*if only I could scream someone will hear me, someone will come*—yet at the same time she knew *he* would hear her—*he'd* be the only one to hear her, the only one who would come. . . .

He would come for her, and he would bring his sword. . . .

He will come for me, and Nan won't sing. . . .

Jenny's hands missed the last holes, and she fell the rest of the way, crashing onto the table beneath. Her battered body felt oddly detached—someone else's body, someone else's pain—and as she crawled over to her bed, she told herself that nothing here was real—*nothing*—not the sudden knocking at her door, not the way it was coming open now, so slowly . . . slowly . . .

"No," she whispered, "no . . ."

And *Malcolm's face—no—Derreck's face—which one—who—*straining her eyes through the agony and the dizziness, seeing him there with the candle held beneath his chin so that he looked dead—dead and ghostly and unreal—

"Jenny," he whispered, and there was fear in his voice, *real* fear, real *concern,* as he glanced back over his shoulder, as he crossed the room and took her hand and tried to get her up.

"Come with me, Jenny. You've got to come—"

"Something's happened," she said numbly. "Something terrible—"

"Yes, I know. That's why I must take you some-where else."

"Where?" she mumbled. "Where are you taking me?"

"A safe place," he whispered. "Trust me."

"Malcolm"—she could hardly get the name out—"I saw . . . Malcolm—" And she was crying, and his dark handsome face swam gently through her tears—"I saw him . . . with his sword—"

"It's all right," he said, "I'm not Malcolm," and she tried to hang back, but he had his arm around her now, and he was guiding her carefully to the door. She saw the stairwell yawning beneath them, and she whimpered in fear, but he hugged her, comforting her, and pressed close to her side as he began leading her down the winding steps.

"Where . . . are we going?" Jenny moved her head against his chest and saw him smiling down at her.

"Ssh . . . don't talk."

And she was so tired, so tired and so terrified, and she was leaning on him, all her weight, as he guided her down and down and down into the darkness, into the nothingness. She felt the floor go level again, and she knew they were going through passageways, and he was being so careful with her, so gentle with her, half carrying her now as she stumbled through the shadows. Not like Derreck, she thought hazily. *I never expected Derreck to be so gentle, not after the way he threatened me. . . .* Her head sank lower onto his chest, and she tried to make herself wake up. All around her Derreck's candle made weird shapes on the walls, and in her mind she could suddenly see that sinister figure again, the sword coming down—*Malcolm . . . you never can tell him apart. . . .*

Jenny began to cry—loud, racking sobs that echoed through the hollow passageways.

"He killed her—I think he killed Nan!"

And Derreck didn't stop, just kept guiding her through the tunnels, and she could feel the dank, spoiled air, and she had the feeling they were going down, down, even deeper beneath the foundations of the castle, and she wasn't walking anymore— she was falling, the candlelight snuffed out, and he was lifting her, carrying her, moving swiftly through the dark.

"Tell me," Jenny pleaded. "Tell me what's happening—"

And "yes," Derreck murmured, his lips soft against her ear. "Yes. Now. I'll tell you."

She thought she heard a door opening. . . .

An empty sound going on and on forever.

"I'm sorry you had to see that, Jenny—sorry you had to see what he's capable of."

"What?" she murmured. "What did you say?"

"Insanity is a family's blackest secret. A family's worst shame. Something to hide and turn away from. Even when it *is* your own brother."

Ice crept through Jenny's veins. She felt faint, but Derreck's grip around her was sure and strong.

"He has his moments of normalcy, of course. Rational moments when he can talk just as you and I are talking now . . . *feeling* moments when he's actually capable of sadness and loneliness and . . . love."

Jenny's heart tore at the words. *Malcolm . . . his kiss . . . I believed him . . . I wanted to . . .*

Derreck's voice sank to a whisper.

"But he never knows . . . when those moments will be. When he might be like other people. He wants to so much, you know. He wants to be just like his brothers . . . like everyone else. But he can't be trusted. Not ever. No one knows what he might be thinking . . . or what he might do next."

"Then . . . I wasn't dreaming . . . it *was* real." Jenny shook her head, tears filling her eyes. "All of it. All those terrible things . . ."

"He knows the castle better than anyone," Derreck's voice echoed hollowly through the dark. "He can go where no one else can. He knows things no one else knows."

His grip tightened, and he pressed Jenny tenderly against him.

"He fell in love with you, you know," Derreck said quietly. "That very first night. That very first time he . . . touched you—"

"Please don't," Jenny murmured. "Derreck, what are we going to do?"

"Ssh . . . you're safe now. Safe with me. . . ."

And then another dark place, darker even than before, Jenny could sense it and see it all at the same time, and she was being lowered down, down by her arms, down, onto a cold wet floor, and it smelled of mildew and damp, and she could hear . . . *water?*

The rain . . . it's the rain I hear—the terrible storm—

Yet in the back of her mind she knew it wasn't the

storm—no thunder, no lightning—just the thick, restless slurp of water. . . .

"Where are we?" she asked, and she was even colder now, something prickling along her skin . . . up her spine . . . filling her heart with sudden fear —"Derreck, where *are* we?"

Groggily she looked up. She could see the spurt of a candle, and she could see Derreck's face, but it seemed so far above her, everything miles and miles above her. . . .

Derreck looked down and smiled. The candle-light cast nervous shadows over his calm, calm face.

"We're in a secret place," he murmured. "Our secret. Yours and mine."

"Derreck—"

"In fact, it's so secret, nobody ever leaves here. Did I forget to tell you that?"

"What are you talking about? What—"

"Don't worry. I won't take the light. I want you to *see* what's happening. It might be . . . entertaining . . . for you. Too bad you won't be able to put it in your story."

"Derreck!"

His face vanished.

Jenny lay there, frozen with shock, unable to comprehend what was happening. *My God . . . did he leave me here?* She raised herself on her elbows and squinted through the gloom, trying to figure out where she was.

She was lying on a ledge.

A narrow stone ledge with steps at one end, leading high up a wall. As Jenny's frightened gaze followed the rise of the stairs, she could see that they ended abruptly, several feet below a small barred doorway near the ceiling. *Someone's behind there—I can feel it . . . watching me, watching to see what I'll do. . . .*

Wincing with pain and dizziness, she sat up the rest of the way and stared around her in disbelief.

The cavern was huge, enclosed on all sides by solid rock, its surfaces darkened with water stains and slime. As Jenny's gaze traveled slowly around the chamber, she could see other ledges jutting out from the walls, each of them located high near the vaulted ceiling, each of them positioned below another barred opening. Straight out from where she lay, pale gray mist rose like steam, showing just a dull glimmer of blackness underneath.

Water . . .

Jenny's eyes widened in dismay.

She could see it now, everywhere, all around her, and she realized she was lying at the very edge of it. She could hear it, lapping softly and hungrily at the walls, and she could see where gaping sections of stone had worn away from the tireless suction of the waves.

"No," she whispered, and then her voice rose in a frantic scream. "Derreck! Come back!"

But of course it *wasn't* Derreck, she knew that now—it *wasn't* Derreck who had carried her through the darkness, comforting her about Nan's murder, holding her so tightly, telling her to trust him—it wasn't Derreck who had talked on and on about madness and torment and Malcolm—

Oh, Malcolm—it was you—talking about your-self—

"Somebody help me! Please help me!"

And at first she thought he was coming back—the sounds echoing around her, of something sliding . . . something opening . . . a footstep on stone . . .

But as she raised her eyes to the doorway above and saw the tall black figure framed there, her heartbeat seemed to stop, and her breath froze in her throat. . . .

"The game's over, Jenny," the executioner whispered. "I win the prize."

23

Jenny's lips moved, but no sound came out.

As the hooded figure gazed down at her, she saw the sword he held in one hand . . . saw the rope he clenched in the other.

"Malcolm," she mumbled at last. "I know it's you. Please don't do this—"

"The tide is coming in," he said, and his voice was so loud in the quiet, so unnaturally loud, yet at the same time so completely and thoroughly calm.

Jenny staggered to her feet, teetering on the slippery ledge. Her mind was jolted into full awareness now, yet numb with terror.

"The tide is coming in," the executioner spoke again. "It comes in very quickly here, you know. Rises very fast. And with the tide come . . . rats. My little friends. Hundreds of them. Swimming and swimming."

Jenny gaped up at him through the shadows. She couldn't move . . . couldn't speak.

"Funny thing about all that exercise," he said casually. "It makes them quite hungry." He stopped and stared off across the water. "Ah—I believe—yes. Here come some now."

Jenny gasped and turned her head. She could hear something—*thought* she could hear something—or was it just in her mind? Tiny legs swimming? Tiny voices squealing?

"Of course you can fight them off for a while," he went on matter-of-factly. "You can even climb the steps, as far as they'll take you, but unfortunately you'll never quite reach the door. Eventually you'll grow tired. And the water will be up over your head. And then you won't be able to fight them off anymore. It might give you something to think about, while you're waiting." He stopped, considering. "Drowning . . . or being eaten alive."

"Why are you doing this!" she shrieked.

"Because of you." His voice echoed hollowly. "Because I want you to stay."

"Let me out of here! Please! I'll do anything, just let me out!"

"Anything?" His voice seemed to smile. "Will you . . . die for me?"

"Oh, God! Somebody help me!"

"Nobody will help you, Jenny. Nobody will even know you've been here. That's the beauty of this particular torture . . . this particular death. Nobody will ever know."

"Oh, please—come back—"

"One more riddle, Jenny. Who am I? Guess the answer before . . . you . . . die."

Jenny's blood turned to ice.

Wit? But it sounded like Malcolm! Or has it been Derreck all along, trying to make me believe it was Malcolm—

She heard the maniacal laugh, going on and on, mocking her from every wall. The only flicker of light shone from the candle on the topmost step. Jenny's mind seemed to tilt, to flash, to burst with some unknown reserve of strength. She stumbled over and climbed to the first step.

There was a noise behind her.

Whirling around, she saw a slick, furry head coming toward her, swimming through the fog.

"Oh, God, no!"

Jenny scrambled up another step. As she slipped, banging her shin, stars exploded behind her eyes and she screamed in pain.

The rat scrambled out of the water and onto the ledge. It hesitated, blinking at her in the half-light. Its eyes glimmered red.

"No . . . no . . ."

Jenny looked around wildly for a weapon. She clawed her way up several more steps and paused there, looking down.

The rat stared at her. Its whiskers quivered, and it raised its nose, sniffing the air.

Jenny wondered if it could smell the blood on her leg.

The rat darted to the bottom step and jumped up without a second's hesitation.

"Please," Jenny sobbed, "somebody help. . . ."

"Oh, Jenny, Jenny, how trusting you are." Above her the voice suddenly spoke again. "In fact, your sweetness is really quite touching."

There was a muffled squeal, and as Jenny looked up in alarm, she saw the executioner extend his black-gloved hand, a rat swinging from it by its tail.

With one quick movement the executioner tossed it down.

Shrieking, Jenny felt it fall across the back of her neck, and as she tried to shake it off, it scurried down her back and along her arm before finally landing on the step at her feet. Shrieking again, Jenny kicked it into the water and watched it swim straight back again to the ledge.

Around her the shadows flared and dipped. Jenny looked up in terror at the one candle and saw that it was down to nearly nothing.

Another rat pulled itself out of the water. Jenny climbed higher and watched the water creep over the bottom step.

"Don't do this!" she screamed. "Come back! *Please!*"

There was only silence. The hooded figure in the doorway might just as well have been another empty shadow.

The water lurched restlessly, swallowing two more steps. Panic-stricken, Jenny moved up as more rats began to climb. A wet, furry body slithered across her shoe, and she kicked the rodent back into the water.

"Help me!" she screamed. "Please—please— don't leave me here!"

"But you *must* stay here," the voice above her murmured.

Jenny looked up wildly into the masked face. The voice sounded detached now . . . infinitely sad. . . .

"This is where *I* must stay," he whispered. "And I get so . . . *lonely . . .*"

Jenny heard something behind her. Whirling around, she squinted through the gloom.

At first she thought she was seeing things.

Tiny pinpoints of light through the fog, blinking through the fog, something shining, bobbing in the fog, then disappearing. . . .

Jenny rubbed her eyes. *I'm imagining it. . . . there's nothing there. . . .*

But there was.

And as she gazed in horror, she began to count—four . . . seven . . . twelve—sleek heads sticking out of the water, swimming toward the steps.

With a rush the water heaved itself over the steps, dousing Jenny in putrid spray. Horrified, she climbed farther and huddled against the steps above. *No, God . . . please . . .*

And they were climbing out now, darting back and forth along the steps, and the ledge was completely covered—submerged in black water—and the rats—swarming, sliding, climbing higher and higher, alert to her fear . . . her blood . . .

I'm really going to die here . . . I'm really going to die this way. . . .

Tears ran down her face, but Jenny didn't even realize she was crying.

She had reached the top step. Water swirled only inches below her feet, creeping higher every second. She could see the executioner on the ledge above her, just out of reach, and she held out her arms to him desperately.

"Help me! Please!"

He didn't move. He didn't speak. He only stood there watching her, as dark and still as the stone walls around him.

There was nowhere else to go now.

All Jenny could do was wait.

Wait for the water . . . the rats . . . death . . .

The cavern seemed to draw in on itself with a long, shuddering sigh. Jenny looked fearfully at the candle.

There was nothing left of it.

It was going out.

"No!"

She heard him laughing . . . a cold, pitiless laugh . . . and as she gazed up at him in total helplessness, she saw him reach slowly for his hood.

"I'm the best, Jenny—*I* am," he sneered, his fingers curling around the black, black fabric. "I'm the one who's kept you guessing all along! I'm the one who touched you in the passageway that very first night . . . and spied behind the tapestry . . . and crept into your room. It's *my* game we've been playing—*my* game—and oh, how much fun it's been to see you fooled! It was *me* you ran from in the woods—*me* you kissed in the dungeon, Jenny —and *me* who threw the knife—just to make you feel my power—just to make you afraid—because you're so *beautiful* when you're afraid. Fear's a funny thing—so much more powerful than love or even hate—because when someone's afraid, they'll do anything, won't they? Promise anything—obey anything—anything at all. Totally in my power—their life in my hands . . ."

He paused a long while. His low, deep laugh shivered coldly through the shadows.

"I'm the one who hides, Jenny. I'm the one who watches in the dark."

And he was pulling the hood away from his head . . . and the light was throbbing, fading, flaring one last time—

"My God . . ." Jenny murmured.

She saw his dark handsome face—*Malcolm? Derreck?*

And the candle went out.

24

"Jenny! Jenny, where are you?"

In the sudden, total blackness Jenny thought she heard a voice calling out to her. It hung in the air for a split instant . . . then melted away.

Jenny huddled there, terrified. She could feel the water over her feet now, sucking at her, pulling at her shoes. She strained her ears through the awful silence, but all she heard were her own racking sobs.

It wasn't real . . . I just wanted it to be . . . but it wasn't real. . . .

"Jenny! Answer me! Where *are* you?"

And the voice came again, distant and dream-like, like some desperate corner of her mind. . . .

"I'm here!" Jenny screamed, even though she knew it was pointless, even though she knew she was only imagining it. She tried to pull herself as far from the edge of the step as she could—far from the lapping waves—the nervous squeals—"I'm here! Help me! Please!"

And *I did imagine it, no one's coming, I'm really going to die*—because the silence was so full, so heavy and final, and she couldn't even hear *him* anymore—him standing above her, calmly watching her die—

"Can you hear me?" Jenny called again, from the depths of her hopelessness. "Somebody? The water's so deep now! *Hurry!*"

At first she thought the walls were caving in. At first, when she heard the horrible groans, she thought the whole chamber was collapsing, and she braced herself, waiting for the roof to come down on her head. *It'll be easier this way . . . I'll be unconscious and I won't feel anything . . .* She stared out numbly into the endless dark, and she thought how much it was like already having her eyes shut, like already being dead. . . . And suddenly there were lights—lights and movement across the cavern—and to Jenny's amazement, two ledges slowly came into focus, two doorways opening high up on opposite walls. . . .

"Jenny!" a voice shouted. "Are you all right?"

"Hurry!" she screamed, and it wasn't a dream—it was *real*—real voices calling her, real people silhouetted there in the openings—"The rats!" Jenny shouted. "Please hurry!"

And there were candles—she could see them now, only brighter—*no, lanterns!*—lanterns in people's hands, and as the cavern filled slowly with light, she instinctively looked above.

The executioner was gone.

Stunned, Jenny tried to concentrate on what was happening around her. She could feel the stealthy rise of water up her legs. She could hear a confusion of yelling, echoes eerily distorted, voices running together, not making any sense.

"Jenny—can you swim to me?"

"Where?" she pleaded. "How can I?"

"Jenny—swim to me! Swim over here!"

And as Jenny focused in on the voice, she drew her breath in sharply. She could see one of the twins, his face in flickering lanternlight, his hand reaching out to her.

"Swim to me! You've got to!"

And she started to answer him, but she was afraid—*afraid*—and before she could do anything, she saw the other figure on the other ledge— *another twin*—with his arm held out to her.

"Jenny!" the first one called. "Come on—you haven't got much time!"

Frozen, Jenny heard the soggy rustling at her feet . . . saw the rats swarming there. She kicked at them in a frenzy, still trying to keep her eyes on the two doorways, on the two exact same faces. . . .

And when the third voice called out to her unexpectedly, it took her a minute to even realize what was happening . . . to search frantically through the fog . . . to find the third ledge on the third wall. . . .

She never expected the third figure to appear. She wasn't prepared for what she saw in the ghostly light of the lantern.

And she thought in that one wild moment that she really *had* gone crazy, that her mind had snapped and pulled her into madness, for she could see all their faces now in a half circle around her—*all* their faces—all *three* of them—

All three . . .

Identical.

"Jenny!" one of them yelled. "It's Malcolm! Jenny—come to me—"

"Don't listen to him!" another shouted. "He's lying! He's not Malcolm—he's a murderer!"

"That's what he *wants* you to believe, Jenny—he'd say *anything* to make you believe that! I'm the *real* Malcolm—I'm the one you can trust!"

"Jenny, it's Derreck!" the third voice called. "I'm closest to you—don't panic—"

"No, Jenny. Come to me."

"How do you know you can trust *him?*"

"He'd say *anything* to confuse you!"

"Stay there, Jenny! I'll come for you!"

"No, Jenny—you'll have a better chance if you swim! Jump into the water and come this way!"

"I can't!" Jenny screamed.

She was sobbing so hard, she could hardly see. The light and fog drizzled together into a sallow mist, and blurry shapes crawled toward her. She moved toward one side of the step, and the voices began shouting louder.

"No, Jenny—don't go to him! He'll kill you!"

"He's lying, Jenny—he's the *real* murderer!"

"His name is Edwyn, Jenny—he's our brother. He's the reason Father called us home. He's insane, and Father's hidden him here for years—only now the house is going to be opened, and he can't hide him anymore—"

"Don't listen to him, Jenny—he's lying—"

"He's a murderer, Jenny! He's killed Nan—and now we know there've been others—"

"What stories, Jenny! He doesn't know what he's talking about!"

"He tried to kill Wit, too—only Nan found me at the tournament and told me. I was trying so hard to get away—I was afraid I wouldn't get back to him in time, but I did!"

"I don't believe you!" Jenny screamed. "It was just a joke—you're all lying to me!"

"Trust me, Jenny. I'd already had a fight with Edwyn before the tournament. He was out of control! You've got to believe me—"

"No, Jenny, don't—"

"I *saw* you!" Jenny went on frantically. "You—*one* of you—with Wit and Nan in that room—you were planning to kill someone—I *heard* you!"

"Nan was going to drug Edwyn tonight so we could sneak him out of the house and get him to a hospital—we knew we might get in trouble, but we were desperate, we didn't know what else to do! We thought if they could just keep him for observation, then Father would be forced to put him somewhere!"

"It's Father's fault—he should have committed Edwyn long ago! But he felt guilty—as if it were *his* fault Edwyn was insane! So he always tried to make it up to him—and he looked the other way when he suspected Edwyn did things!"

"So we broke off, Jenny! Went our separate ways! When Father begged us to come home this time, we never realized how bad Edwyn had gotten. Father can't handle him anymore! He's finally more terrified of Edwyn than he is of being old and alone! It's true, Jenny—listen to me!"

"Yes, Jenny, *listen!* He *is* insane—insane enough to be smarter than anyone! To make up lies—to make you believe him!"

"Believe *me,* Jenny—"

"No! He'd say anything to save himself—"

"He's the murderer, all right, but he's not crazy! He knows exactly what he's doing—"

"Hurry, Jenny—*swim!*"

"No, don't move—I'll come for you!"

"Stop it!" Jenny sobbed.

And she could feel the rat slithering against her arm—the sudden, sharp pain in her elbow as she screamed and jerked away—

"Jenny!"

"I'm going after her—"

"No—you can't swim!"

"Wait—look out!"

And water was splashing—voices shouting—the restless tide hurling upward toward the high dark ceiling. Trickles of light seeped through the fog, turning it a jaundiced yellow. Jenny caught only a glimpse of thrashing arms among the waves, and everything seemed strangely surreal—the numbing cold, the water up to her waist now, the quick, slippery bodies swimming furiously on all sides of the step . . . *There's no way out for me . . . no way out . . .*

She slipped into the water, and there were things swimming around her, squirming and slithering, and *oh, God I don't feel anything anymore, please let it happen fast—* She opened her mouth and swallowed a huge gulp of water— *Just let me pass out, I don't want to feel anything anymore—*

"Take my hand, Jenny—*take it!*"

Her eyelids fluttered open. Foul water choked her, and she sputtered helplessly, fighting to breathe. Someone was beside her—grabbing her shirt—and frantically she tried to swim away. As something came down hard upon her head, she plunged deep beneath the waves, her lungs bursting in agony.

"Hold on to me!" And the voice was miles away, fuzzy beneath layers and layers of water . . . and she was drifting . . . drifting . . .

"Take my hand! Jenny—"

She could see the water churning, dark shapeless figures locked together, twisting and turning, and the voice again— someone pulling on her clothes, pulling her on and on and on through a watery grave. . . .

"Take my hand!"

Gasping, her head broke the surface, and she fought desperately for air. And she could see the vague outline of a hand just above her, and she could see the thin line of scar across the width of the palm . . . *"But scars give us integrity, don't you think?"*

"Derreck," she mumbled.

And she put her hand in his because she was so tired . . . so very tired . . . because she didn't have any other choice. . . .

"I've got you," he said to her, hauling her up, holding her in his arms. "Don't worry . . . I've got you now. . . ."

Jenny nodded dumbly. She pulled away from him and lowered her eyes and stared down at his left hand.

But there was no scar.

It had only been a shadow.

25

No!" Jenny screamed.

Wildly she began to struggle, hitting and kicking, while the arms around her tightened and tried to hold her still.

"Jenny—stop it! It's all right—it's me!"

She managed to jerk free for an instant. Striking out, she heard his exclamation of pain, and then she was being pinned again, tighter than ever.

"Dammit, Jenny—stop! It's me! Malcolm!"

"Let me go!"

"I can't let you go—we've got to get out of here!"

Before she could answer, a body pulled itself out of the water and up onto the ledge beside them. As an identical face appeared beside Malcolm, Jenny stared at it in dismay.

"You all right?" he asked curtly. He looked Jenny over with one quick glance, then pulled on Malcolm's arm. "*You* all right?"

"I've been better."

"I told you not to jump in—I knew I couldn't save both of you."

"What was I supposed to do—let him drown you from behind?"

His brother stared at him, then gave a slow wry smile. "Nice fighting. Even if he *did* get away."

"It was either that or let him drown *me.*" Malcolm gave Jenny a push toward the doorway, but she immediately balked.

"No! I won't—"

"We don't have time to stand around here arguing." Malcolm glanced at his brother. "Tell her I'm Malcolm. I'm *not* the crazy one—"

"Debatable," his brother murmured.

"And this isn't the time for jokes!" Malcolm gave him a look. "Edwyn's totally out of control. Jenny, you'll have to trust me."

"For God's sake, why should she trust *any* of us after what she's been through?" his brother said irritably. "If she won't come, we'll just have to carry her."

"Derreck," Malcolm said, fighting for patience, looking from his brother to Jenny and back again. "Jenny, *this* is Derreck. And I know what he just said is absolutely true—you don't have any reason to believe us, but—"

"But"—Derreck lifted his head, frowning, sniffing the air—"that's not fog coming in now. That's smoke. Get the hell out of here!"

Jenny didn't have time to think. Malcolm and Derreck both took hold of her, determinedly propelling her up steps and down a dark, drafty hall.

Smoke curled stealthily along the passage, stinging her eyes, burning the back of her throat. She was soaked and shivering, and her arm throbbed where the rat had bitten her. As they rounded a curve, a wave of smoke descended upon them, so suddenly, so thick, that for one frightening moment she couldn't even see the boys beside her.

"Malcolm?" she asked and felt his arm tighten around her.

"This way! Come on!"

They were running now, pushing blindly through the heavy pall of smoke. Without warning she felt Derreck brake to a halt and heard the carefully controlled panic in his voice.

"He's set fire to the tunnel—we'll never get out this way. We'll have to go up."

"Are we trapped?" Jenny whispered, but Malcolm gave her a quick, reassuring smile.

"If we can make it to the east tower, there's another way down. It'll take us to an underground tunnel."

"And out," Derreck muttered. "And away from this hellhole."

Malcolm turned and grabbed Jenny as a fit of coughing overtook her.

"Here," Derreck said to him. "Use your shirt."

Jenny watched as both boys stripped out of their wet shirts. Malcolm handed his to Jenny and pressed it over her nose and mouth. Derreck was already moving again, leading them deeper into the swirling black air.

It seemed they went forever.

All Jenny was aware of was the acrid taste in her

throat and the tears running down her cheeks and Malcolm's gray shadow ahead of her as they ran through the twisting darkness. As wet air hit her at last, Jenny gasped and bent her head back, breathing in the rain, looking gratefully up into the raging, open sky.

They were on the battlements.

Lightning ripped savagely through the boiling black night, and rain lashed down on them as they hurried along the slippery walkways. Beneath them the castle shuddered with every clap of thunder, and through the slitted windows of a turret, Jenny could already see smoke and tongues of flame licking up the walls.

Malcolm let go of her hand and wiped distractedly at his face. His cheeks were streaked with smoke and dirt, and as his twin paused beside him, Jenny could see burns swelling across the bare skin of Derreck's chest. Malcolm bent forward, taking in deep gulps of air. Derreck turned away, then immediately stiffened and pointed toward the sky.

"Malcolm—over there!"

The two figures were silhouetted sharply against the storm—Edwyn and Sir John—both of them up on the narrow ledge of the wall, both of them struggling. Edwyn had one arm around his father's throat, the other clutched around a sword, and his shrill laughter rose over the wild, wild wind.

"Give me the girl!" he shouted. "I want Jenny—and you can have . . . our dear father."

Derreck's gaze was cold and steady.

Malcolm pressed against him, his voice dangerously calm.

"You should know by now," Malcolm said. "That's no exchange."

"He's right, Edwyn!" Sir John looked up into his son's contorted face. "They hate me—and they have every right to!"

"I'll kill him!" Edwyn snarled. "He's of no use to me!"

"It's over, Edwyn," Sir John said wearily, and his body sagged against the strength of his son. "I've spent my whole life trying to protect you—I've sacrificed everything—including the love of my other sons—for your well-being!"

"My well-being!" Edwyn's laugh was pitiless. "It had nothing to do with me! You felt *guilty* for fathering a freak! You didn't want to be *alone!* They all left you, but I *couldn't!* You kept me here— hidden away—"

"For your own good!" Sir John cried. "A menace to yourself and society, but still my son! I pitied you! I protected you! I pretended everything was good and right, even when I finally suspected the disgusting truth! And then—*still*—I forgave you!"

Sir John's voice trailed away. A laugh rose from his throat, empty of humor . . . and of hope.

"I never wanted to know how you got out of the castle. . . . I was terrified to think you might have killed or that you would kill again! I only knew that no one could ever suspect you if they never knew you existed."

He stiffened again, his head straining back in Edwyn's merciless grip.

"God forgive me, you *are* my son. But so were the others, and they despise me now. It's over, Edwyn.

Do it quickly. For you . . . for the sons I neglected. God knows I deserve revenge from all of you."

Edwyn's face convulsed in fury.

As a hideous shriek filled the sky, Jenny saw Sir John fall forward onto the stones. Edwyn stood there alone, his sword lifted in his hand, his body poised on the edge of the wall. He seemed to be hanging there, curiously suspended, and as Jenny saw the slow look of surprise creep over his face, she also saw the hilt of a dagger protruding from the center of his chest.

He screamed all the way down.

He screamed until he hit the moat and the rushing water closed over him.

For an endless moment the three of them stood there. Jenny saw Malcolm's frozen face . . . and Derreck's hand lifted at his side.

"Jesus," Malcolm whispered. "Jesus, Derreck . . ."

"I told you," Derreck said, and as he turned to Jenny, she could hear the faint, faint trembling in his voice. "I never miss."

26

Crackling tongues of flame licked the sky.

As a huge crash sounded from one of the towers, a blanket of smoke boiled out, bringing with it the smell of burning timbers and scorched stone.

"Come on!" Derreck shouted. "Hurry!"

"You can't leave him here!" Jenny cried. Immediately she ran over to Sir John and gently rolled his prone body over.

"Let them go, my dear," the old man looked up at her, his haggard face crumpled with weariness. "After all the trouble I've brought them . . . it's better this way . . ." He reached out to Malcolm. "Quick, find your brother, find Wit."

"Don't worry about Wit," said Derreck. "He's safe. Let's go!"

"Malcolm!" Jenny begged.

She saw the boys exchange looks. Derreck swore

under his breath and ran back, hoisting his father onto his shoulders.

"I don't know if we can make it—that tower's like a furnace—"

"We can make it," Malcolm said quickly. He grabbed Jenny's hand and plunged ahead through the smoke.

Jenny could hardly breathe. As they entered the close confines of the tower, smoke boiled up from below, engulfing them in darkness. Heat poured from the walls, and every step was like burning coals. Jenny kept the shirt pressed over her nose, and as she glanced back, she saw that Derreck had wrapped his shirt around Sir John's face. Jenny couldn't tell if Sir John was breathing or not. She kept tight hold of Malcolm's hand and followed him blindly down the winding stairs.

She felt as if she was passing out. As the bitter taste of smoke filtered through the wet shirt, Jenny swooned and stumbled, falling sideways against the wall. She was scarcely aware of being lifted, of being carried. All she knew was the impossible blackness swirling around her and the crash of burning rubble and the sparks swirling like fireworks through the murky shadows . . .

"Malcolm," she whispered.

"We'll make it, Jenny—just hold on."

"I . . . can't . . ."

"Yes. Yes, you can."

She slipped away from him. For an eternity she floated through hazy memories and nightmares, faces swimming in and out of her mind's vision. *Sir John . . . the twins . . . Wit . . . Nan . . . Edwyn . . .*

She was standing within a three-way mirror, and a dark handsome face gazed back at her from every side. She could see their lips moving . . . could hear them whispering, softly, like the whisper of the rain. . . .

With a gasp Jenny woke up. Rain was falling on her face, and as she turned her head, she realized she was lying in tall grass. Disoriented, she raised herself on her elbows and looked around. Silhouetted against the raging night, Worthington Hall was a blazing inferno. She could see a shadow standing only a few feet away, and as she struggled to her knees, Sir John turned around and regarded her with a dazed stare.

"They're gone, you know. All of them. My boys . . . gone."

Jenny looked back at him, not fully understanding.

"Malcolm," she mumbled. "Derreck . . ."

"Gone."

He turned away and gazed for several minutes at the flaming horizon.

"It's right that they should go. How much more could I ask of them?" He shook his head distractedly; his smile was bittersweet. "People will come soon—with help and questions and good intentions. My boys have never much cared for . . . inconveniences."

Jenny looked around herself in bewilderment. She saw rocks and sloping fields. She saw woods below them and the deserted streets of the fair.

"But . . . where?" she asked slowly.

"To live their lives. The lives I've ruined for

them all these many years. I'll . . . never see them again."

Jenny heard the catch in his voice. He turned once more to face her, and the rain streamed down his cheeks, mingling with his tears.

"But *you* will, my dear," he murmured. "I've no doubt about that."

"Me?" Jenny's heart was full. She wanted to know so much, to understand so much, but all she could do was watch him, the eerie smile on his face, the way his eyes grew large and empty.

"One good thing in the midst of bad." Sir John laughed softly and nodded. "One very good thing. And we must always pursue . . . the good things . . . in our lives. Musn't we?"

His voice faded. Jenny could hear sirens in the far, far distance. Sir John stumbled away from her, and Jenny knew he'd forgotten she was even there.

She looked down at the ground beside her and saw what was left of Malcolm's shirt.

She picked it up and held it gently against her cheek.

Beneath the storm-ravaged sky, Worthington Hall fell gloriously into ashes.

Epilogue

"No more vacations with Dad." Jenny shook her head. "I mean it, Mom. None. Ever. Promise me. Don't even bring it up."

She watched her mother drop the mail onto the kitchen counter and begin to sort through it.

"Okay, so I was wrong." Mom sighed. "I thought it'd be a good idea. I thought maybe he'd changed."

"Dad's never going to change. You should know that by now."

"Well, I at least thought he was more responsible! I still can't believe he just went off and left you there in that horrible place! And then to think it—it—"

"It's okay, Mom," Jenny said quickly, wishing they could change the subject. "It's been two whole months since the trip, anyway—I don't know why you keep bringing it up."

"The place caught fire, Jenny!"

"But I got out!" Jenny reassured her with what she hoped was a convincing smile. "See? I'm here, aren't I? I got out."

"But that poor man who helped you . . . the one who led you out of there—"

"Sir John," Jenny mumbled. "Mr. Worthington."

"Yes, the dear man." Mom's eyes teared up. "What a brave thing for him to do!"

Jenny gripped the edge of her chair with both hands. A gentle rush went through her head, and for one bittersweet moment she could hear the sound of flames and crumbling walls, the flowing of rain, the murmur of Malcolm's voice. . . .

"Jenny?" her mother broke in. "Did you ever hear anything else about poor Mr. Worthington? Did he ever start talking again or respond to *anything* in the hospital? It's so sad, the terrible shock he must have suffered."

"I . . . I don't know." *I told the police Sir John got me out. I never told them, never told anyone, about Derreck or Malcolm or Wit . . . Sir John asked me not to . . . begged me not to . . . and so I told Dad the boys weren't even there when the fire started, that they'd left the castle the day before and I never knew where they'd gone. . . .*

"Poor man," Mom said again. "To have your house—everything—destroyed."

They never found Nan . . . never found Edwyn . . . but how could they, even if they'd known— layers and layers of scorched stone and smoldering timbers caved in upon secret underground tunnels . . . leaving no clues, no suspicions . . . just a crazy

212

*old house that caught fire and burned and wasn't
that a shame, the police had said, a damn shame,
but a blessing really, the place all rotting away, just
an accident waiting to happen—*

"Jenny?" Mom's voice was sharp, and with an
effort Jenny pulled herself back to the present.

"Sorry, Mom, what did you say?"

"I said maybe we can think of something really
exciting for you to do next summer. So you won't
be bored."

In spite of herself Jenny chuckled. "Mom . . . I
think I'm beginning to like boring. In fact, I want to
be a boring person from now on. How about I just
stay home and spend my summer at the mall?"

"Hmmm." Mom gave a knowing look, then
glanced down at the stack of letters still clutched in
her hand. "We don't need any more bills around
here—the mailman leaves plenty now as it is.
Oh—here's something. *Not* a bill. Looks like it's
for you."

Jenny reached out and caught the envelope her
mother tossed her. She didn't recognize the hand-
writing on the front.

"Who's that?" Mom asked, smiling. "A secret
admirer?"

Jenny stared down at it, puzzled. "I don't know.
There's no return address. As a matter of fact"—
she held it up and frowned—"it doesn't even have
a stamp."

"No?" Mom sounded only mildly interested.
"Must have sneaked past the machines. When *I* try
to do that, it always comes back postage due."

She opened the refrigerator door and began

pulling out lettuce and cold cuts. Jenny turned the envelope over and slit it with her finger.

The writing looked as if it'd been done by a child.

The letters were big and scrawly, and there were little doodles and cartoons interspersed between the words.

The message was short.

Only four lines.

> DON'T TRY TO RUN
> DON'T TRY TO HIDE
> YOU WON'T GET FAR
> WE'RE RIGHT OUTSIDE

"Jenny—what is it? Where are you going?"

Mom straightened up in alarm as Jenny dashed over and flung open the back door.

"Jenny? Honestly, honey, I wish you'd help me with lunch and quit playing games—"

Jenny looked down the driveway . . . to the car parked alongside the curb.

Then she clutched the paper to her heart and started laughing.

About the Author

Richie Tankersley Cusick loves to read and write scary books. Richie enjoys writing when it is rainy and gloomy outside, and likes to have a spooky soundtrack playing in the background. She writes at a desk which originally belonged to a funeral director in the 1800s and which she believes is haunted. Halloween is one of her favorite holidays. She and her husband decorate the entire house, which includes having a body laid out in state in the parlor, lifesize models of Frankenstein's monster, the figure of Death to keep watch, and a scary costume for Hannah, their dog. A neighbor recently told them that a previous owner of the house was feared by all of the neighborhood kids and no one would go to the house on Halloween.

Richie is the author of *Vampire, Fatal Secrets, The Mall, Silent Stalker,* and the novelization of *Buffy, the Vampire Slayer.* She and her husband, Rick, live outside Kansas City, where she is currently at work on her next novel.